"Provocative . . . Chua's novel glitters."
—Anderson Tepper, *Time Out New York*

"The writing is tightly drawn. Calculated. Unblinking . . . Like surrendering to a beautiful body you know will be cruel to you, Lawrence Chua reveals the story in the edgy soft logic akin to dreams and memory. . . . What Chua manages so brilliantly, even beyond the dense, breathcatching beauty of the writing, is to set a broad historical context within which we experience their relationship. . . . Chua reminds us that our desires live within a dense and sometimes violent complication."
—Thérèse Murdza, *The Lambda Book Report*

"Gritty and revealing . . . The images are often graphic and disturbing, giving this story a hard and realistic edge. . . . Well recommended."
—Shirley N. Quan, *Library Journal*

"Chua's ability to veer from the novel's epileptically paced present-tense, first-to-second-person narration to cocaine-fueled, geopolitical, transhistorical mega-insights is heady."
—Alvin Lu, *San Francisco Bay Guardian*

"Chua is interested in the dangers of romantic obsession and the difference between personal and national identity, but his big themes are overshadowed by warm, concise prose and a simple tale of two lovers in a faraway land." —Robert L. Pela, *The Advocate*

"A vibrant and breathtaking writer of literary prose . . . Like the novels of Nadine Gordimer and Doris Lessing, *Gold by the Inch* attempts to wed the personal with the political, the emotional with the cultural. . . . **Boldly literary and often shocking in its simplicity** . . . Disturbing and deeply moving." —Michael Bronski, *The Guide*

gold by the inch

gold by the inch

lawrence chua

grove press/new york

7 © 1992 by Controversy Music, administered by WB Music Corp. ASCAP. Composed by Prince. Co-written by Lowell Fulsom and Jimmy McCrackin. Published by Powerforce Music/Budget Music BMI.

Published simultaneously in Canada
Printed in the United States of America

FIRST PAPERBACK EDITION

Library of Congress Cataloging-in-Publication Data
Chua, Lawrence.
Gold by the inch / Lawrence Chua.
p. cm.
ISBN 0-8021-3649-4 (pbk.)
I. Title.
PS3553.H777G6   1998
813'.54—dc21   97-36075
CIP

DESIGN BY LAURA HAMMOND HOUGH

Grove Press
841 Broadway
New York, NY 10003

99 00 01 02   10 9 8 7 6 5 4 3 2 1

for madame lim siew moi

"It is part of morality not to be at home in one's own home."
—Theodor W. Adorno, *Minima Moralia*

There will be a new city with streets of gold
The young so educated—they will never grow old
And there will be no death
4 with every breath,
The voice of many colors sings a song
That's so bold . . .
Sing it while we watch them fall—

♀, 7

gold by the inch

construction → death
feminization → subversion o'
death
(painting finger-
nails red

THE STRAITS TIMES, SINGAPORE, April 28, 1990—
Wijit Potha, a 28-year-old migrant worker from Thailand, was found
dead this morning by fellow workers who shared his spare living quarters
near a construction site at Tanjong Pagar. A colleague said Mr. Wijit
had complained of a headache and taken a half day off, but seemed fine at
dinner. An autopsy found the cause of death to be heart failure. So far
this year, 18 Thais, nearly all of them construction workers with no pre-
vious symptoms of illness, have died in their sleep in Singapore.

A number of Thai and Singaporean doctors studying the problem
have no more convincing explanation for the deaths, which are apparently
not uncommon in northeastern Thailand, where most of the workers are
from. They are best known there as "lai tai," or "nightmare deaths,"
and are usually put down to supernatural causes.

The mysterious deaths have provoked some Thai workers here, as
well as some men in rural northeastern Thailand, to paint their finger-
nails red. The idea is to dupe murderous "widow ghosts" who are hunt-
ing for husbands into thinking the men are really women, and thus letting
them live.

3

U.S. $1 = 25 baht

[handwritten annotation: city = corrupt, superficial, decadent]

Hear that?

This is the sound of a city I once knew, slowed down to a dull innuendo. Last night just when the plane touched down it all came back to me. Motors humming down streets dirty with memory. Sleepless children locked in a cradle of indecipherable exchanges. The greasy throb of love songs sucked off crumbling pavement. A landscape heaving with arrogance and possibility. Each face that passes a muffled promise of salvation. The city as bitch, a sonorous lullaby of hungry flies. Garlands rotting at the feet of gods and sex tourists. A real piece of work. You and me sitting by the windows in Mahbunkrong dipping our straws in iced coffee and making crawling worms out of the paper wrappers. The wind blowing off the river like a common suggestion. Then the monuments. Then the buildings. . . .

I wrote this on the back of a postcard crossing the Menam:
The image lasts all the way across.

It's spring, and I'm twenty-three.

You think there are no seasons here, right? Just the heat. I'm here to tell you otherwise. Even after ten years, I can still tell the difference between the days. I can feel the gradations between the mess of the rainy afternoons. Today I can feel the wind kissing the back of my neck, welcoming me home.

I'm wearing a black suit but it's not real. It's a skillful copy anyone can buy for 2500 baht, with the authentic label sewn in like an afterthought. It's not the most appropriate thing to wear in the heat, I know. But I wanted to wear it. It makes me look different. That never seemed important to me before but it is now. Here. People wear suits in this weather all the time. But not like this one. It's black and the wool is heavy. Woven shut. I should be sweating, but I'm too anxious.

On the ferry again. Following someone else's footsteps. Shit. I'm wide awake.

The back of my mouth still tastes like Darkie toothpaste, the last thing that went past my lips this morning. My skin is clear and damp. It's too hot to be wearing this suit, but I am. There's nearly a handful of pomade in my hair, making it stick to my scalp. Excessive, I know, but I prefer it this way because it makes my head look smaller. As it is, my head is too big for the rest of my body. It's obvious, but in these waking moments, I don't think about it too much. It's probably the least of my worries.

He's a hustler. A hooker as opposed to a whore. You know the difference, right? Just because you give a blow job in a phone booth doesn't make you a call girl. We met up north in Bangkok. Do you want to hear that we met at a disco and he left his john alone to come stand next to me. That later, after the introductions were done, we went back to my hotel room and brushed our lips against each other. That it was the purest kiss I can remember, transcendent of our roles that night. That I wanted to see him naked but could only get my eyes halfway open. That we kissed and necked for at least two hours and fell asleep hard. That the next day I gave him money, but he wouldn't accept it.

Let me try again. Luk, my brother, is working here and I'm visiting. You could say my brother is a signature: the Architect. A name appended at the corners of the buildings he plans. It's been a long time since I've been back to this part of the world. We call it home, even though I was born across the border, a full day's train ride away. I've come back at Luk's invitation. There are a few hundred dollars and two credit cards in my wallet, but mostly this is Luk's party. Anyway, he is working here, and he takes me to his favorite brothel.

The little brass plate on the teak door says LES BEAUX. It's a small piss-elegant bar in the Metro shopping center, where the manager greets us like the suits we're wearing and projects slides of boys on the wall. This one is nice, that one is nicer. All of this makes me uncomfortable in ways I've never thought about. My teeth are chattering, and I wrap my arms around myself to keep from shaking much harder. Luk thinks the air-conditioning is getting to me and says we're in the coldest country on earth. The manager laughs as if coldness were the thing. The thing to be considered in place of the anticipation that really makes me shiver. Luk smiles back and nurses his gin and tonic. I like this one, I can hear him say, and there he is, sitting next to us. His nickname is a cheap candy: Olé. He's small and dark, and he likes me better

Commodities
&
social relations

than he likes Luk. I feel protective of him. He's three years younger than I am, and he's from the south like us. I even know the small town he names, a piece of dust on the southern railway line. I ask him why he's not in school. And there I betray our fundamental difference. I betray how long I've been away. What a stupid question. I promise to spend the rest of my life here in repentance, but only if I can fall in love. Let's go, Luk nudges me. Then, politely, as if it's without meaning:

—Is there anyone you're interested in?

There's someone, dressed all in black, sitting at the far end of the bar. Ambivalent eyes. A nose that looks as if it's been pounded flat between them. Lips floating in blemishless autumn skin. A face stolen from a boxing ring. But it's the wind glazing his eyes that compels me to ask.

—How about him?

—That's Thong, the manager says. —He's busy. Call tomorrow. Maybe then.

No prescription necessary. You should know that I'm taking Percodans. Or that's what I asked for. The pharmacist seemed to know what I was talking about. They don't really have those here. Instead, he gives me the substitute drug Burroughs Wellcome manufactures. You can't buy this in America anymore because the FDA discovered it causes birth defects. But they had so many of them manufactured already, it would have been a shame to destroy them. They have pills here that no one even knows the names of yet. You can buy Quaalude here also. Or something like it, anyway. Luk prefers them to my fake narcotics. Sometimes it feels like he is a whole generation older than me. Several months later, half his face will have frozen. The doctor will say it's Bell's

9

palsy. But right now that's not important. Right now I'm taking Percodans and feeling very very . . . content.

The air doesn't move at night. I'm sitting at a bar. There are naked children dancing on the bar, dripping hot wax all over themselves, entwining themselves indifferently in each other's arms. The eyes watching them are shiny with appreciation. If you go down the street, there are bars manned by girls. There is the one where Dang, this woman we met last night on the dance floor at Mars, works, pulling razor blades out of her vagina. The boys on the bar, the woman under the lights, the boy with synthetic opiates dancing through his veins: we are all too numb to be startled.

An Instamatic snapshot, redolent, fresh from process. In this picture I'm sitting at another bar. A nice bar. Nice because you can't tell who's on the game. Nice because nobody talks about money and love in the same sentence. It's called the Milk Bar. Muk, the decaying queen who appointed herself my surrogate mother the minute she found out how old I was, owns the place. The tiny room is fitted with zebra skins and an American fifties retro theme. After midnight it fills up with the fresh faces of the nation's young elite. They may be wearing nothing flashier than jeans and a T-shirt, but from their arrived English to their discreetly confident gestures, they register their origins in the oldest and most respectable families in the nation. The lost tribe of the Beautiful, returning from Swiss boarding schools and rude northern winters, always comes here to roost. Foreign faces, red with sun or shame I cannot tell, project themselves continuously at the other bars and clubs on the street. But they have no place here, giving the bar an exclusive air, even though the doors are unguarded, always open to the warm night. The appearance of free entry. Muk is frequently behind the bar, performing her second job: chopping up cocaine.

—Don't call it dope. This is my medication.

Frankly, I hate the shit. It makes me talk too much, and I hate to talk. My best friend for the last week, Boi, has his arm around my shoulders. Me. A quiver of light. A small pop before the click of the shutter. The flash blots out the skin's history, erasing the seams and the holes and the grease. You can tell by the hidden damage that it's been one hell of a party so far. I could lie here. Tell you how I earned every scar in this photo in an Armani suit and champagne haze. But why say "ravished" when you can say "fucked up"? Anyway, I am rather fond of this shot. Besides the fact that I actually look kind of cute in this picture, what I like most about it is the feeling it gives you. You the voyeur. That you're part of something you never had.

Before you leave the apartment for the last time. Before the taxi shuttles you across day-old snow to the airport. Before you step on the plane, you know you have left something behind. You feel it nagging at you even as the plane pushes up and nudges you into sleep. You sort through the things you have packed up in a cardboard box. Books. Clothes. A telephone. Gathering dust in a storage room. Then you remember. It's him. You left him behind. Someone you thought you could never leave. You push the back of your head farther into the scratchy paper pillowcase behind you. Farther into uncertainty. Feel something warm. Light and terrible. But you still feel him. Inside you. You can still hear the messages he left on your machine the day you left. His voice, pleading first. Then angry. Agitated that he still wanted you back.

The next night, after dinner, you call the brothel. The manager says Thong is busy. Then he tells you to hold on a minute. You can hear his palm against the mouthpiece of the phone, suffocating you. His voice returns, full of promise.

—Come by tonight at eleven.

How could he know so much about you? There is no mistaking your profile glimpsed from the front table at the Milk Bar. This face held in a cradle made of uncalloused hands. Like a face you've seen hundreds of times. Brown and tired. No one will address you as anything but a returning son. That is, until you open your mouth. You wish your syntax was a slab of clay. Wet and blank. Ready to be engraved. But your voice already betrays ruin and impurities. A few casual encounters, the man cutting papayas on the street, the woman ladling soup over noodles, will look surprised when you pick over certain words in their speech that you can't remember.

Oh, just one thing. We don't say brothel here. We say bar.

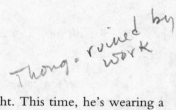
Thong = ruined by work

He is waiting for us that night. This time, he's wearing a blue shirt. His mouth is a rude callus. His eyes are so indifferent it makes his smile even more devastating. He holds my hand in front of his manager.

At twenty-three—would you believe this has never happened to me before? I want to tell him a lot of things. I want to say: I've held that job before. Or something like it anyway. How do you think I came up with the plane fare? You think I come over here every year like some chinky dentist's son? I worked hard to get back here. I want to tell him: This job will take you nowhere. But why kid ourselves when we're living proof of a bigger truth. This job will take you everywhere.

At twenty-three—would you believe I've never been with anyone like him before and it feels like I've been with too many? I get restless, counting and remembering. What do I mean by that, like him? Like *me*.

At twenty-three—would you believe I'm paying him or, more accurately, Luk is paying him. For what? To hold my hand. To escort me around to our favorite bars and discos. To play with the revolving doors at Peppermint, to disappear for two minutes

Never been w/another Asian

LAWRENCE CHUA

and come back with a rose for me. To tell me he loves me. To conspire on a clean mattress. All in one night. To kiss me, like we do here, barely touching his face to mine, inhaling deeply.

But I don't need to make up any excuses. This is none of your business anyway.

You were not born in a garden. But you replay the scenarios of creation and lost innocence over and over again. Even knowing that from where you came there wasn't far to fall. Somewhere on the way down, it is raining and you are twelve. You cut the last few periods of school and take the train home. It is already dark. You're looking out the window, straining to see the landscape. What little you see is overlaid by the reflection of your face, looking at the man in the aisle across from you. He is in an unimaginative gray suit with chalk stripes. His hand is in his lap, and in the window you can see he is kneading his crotch. You turn to him and ask Can I help you? but deliver it perhaps a little too aggressively. He says no and gets all quiet. You go back to looking out the window looking at him, thinking perhaps you're mistaken, perhaps you did imagine it all anyway. But there he is again, pushing on the triangle of his scratchy lap. Are you sure you don't want some help, mister? It's the mister that does him in. He motions for you to come over and you settle in the seat next to him, getting a grip on his enormous piece. Let's go into the toilet, you suggest. The car is empty but for safety's sake you go in first; he follows a heartbeat behind. I want to blow you, you say, and make him sit on the aluminum sink. It smells of piss and ammonia but you take his pink circumcised dick out from behind a plastic zipper and dry-cleaned wool. It

14

tastes salty you get the head wet let it rest on your lips he doesn't move you push forward touch his balls with your teeth. He whistles. You are a piece of work. You look up. Can't believe your luck, can you, mister? He reaches for your pants you push his hand with the wedding ring away. No. Just let me blow you. But the ammonia is getting to you. Let's go somewhere else and do this. Your place? he asks. You laugh. My mom's at home, are you crazy? You know this motel. Will he spring for a room? He thinks about it for a while. Sure. You go back to your separate seats. It is another half hour until the train docks, and you spend the ride looking out the window again looking at him and thinking how ugly he is. Two minutes before your stop you sit down next to him and say it. Sorry, you say. Sorry, wrong number. You get off the train and he's right behind you as the train pulls away. Leaving you both there on the platform. I'll give you twenty. I'll give you thirty. OK, fifty. No. No way. I said, No. He is standing incredulous at the station as you walk into shuttered storefronts and gray dust. Mister: he could be dead now for all you know. The last words on his lips were numbers.

Here's what I want you to do. This is the costume I want you to wear. This is what I'm into. My thing. You know. You are young, driven by poverty like every generation to do this. But you've fallen in love with me.

We have so much in common.

I pack the bills into the hotel stationery lightly, scribble his name on the front. I leave it tucked into the English phrase book he's brought with him. I want him to leave it behind him, but he doesn't.

If the city is dead. If the city one day stopped breathing. Up and choked on its own putrid sweat and fumes. If the city is a corpse then you and Luk are on one of its hardening arteries. A klong being filled in with concrete. The site of a new office complex he is building in Siam Square. The sun slips. Tumbles into rain clouds. Deep shade drawn over wicked radiance. Somewhere south of heaven. You watch cranes swivel oblivious in the mud. Luk points out the foundations being laid, his finger tracing intrusions across the sky. The housing and office complex is entered through a supermarket and a series of boutiques. At the corner is a bank. And, of course, there is the *sala phra phum,* the little altar built to house the spirits of the land the building will displace. A little monument to civilization. A little monument to barbarism. Even though his voice barely registers above a whisper, you know Luk is proud of his work. As proud as any other craftsman plying his trade here.

At last Saturday's market in Chatuchak Park you watched a girl with a perm and Chanel backpack weaving through the baskets of celadon plates caged monkeys limbless beggars tin cups rattling pink locusts frying in oil. Before she became a shadow in the crowd she was a needle lacing a wound, all the while talking to her boyfriend on a cellular phone. Tonight you watch an

16

City = site of contradictions

elephant trundle down Thanon Rama I. Elephant swinging her creased, dusty ass down the boulevard, negotiating the evening crush of expensive automobiles. Black mahout on black elephant. Hannibal crossing the Alps: premodern. Black mahout on black elephant in urban traffic jam: postmodern. Black mahout on black elephant taking her own sweet time: antimodern. The city as a place of averted collisions. Beyond a throttle. Beyond a choke. The city of perpetual gridlock.

This city could fool you easy. Last night your taxi driver asked if you were Teochew. Ten years ago all the cabdrivers in this city were Teochew. Today they're all Thai. He smiled back at you resentfully with this bit of information. Don't think he doesn't know the difference between you.

The fence around the perimeter of the building site is engraved with the name of the construction company. Trong Bi Construction and Development, Limited. You know what *Trong Bi* means. The sounds instigated by symbols. Cyphers imitating the crown of a heart and a fish hook. *Lieow kwa. Lieow sai. Trong Bi.* Go straight ahead. In the nineteenth century, green lights used to mark the brothels in Sampeng Lane, the city's Chinatown. Now red lights signal the enterprise of bodies.

This country is changing fast. So fast sometimes it feels like you're standing in a centrifuge, knees wobbling at the center of the world. When you used to live here, this was just some dingy sideshow. Your prospects were limited. Now they're endless.

Perhaps if you two didn't return as architect and tourist you'd be stuck down there. Shoveling cement over wet sand. Perhaps. You dream of moving back to live, but even as the thought cakes in your throat you know that living is not possible. The tin walls you were born in have become unbearable, their comfort something to endure. The price of every air-conditioned convenience

convenience — even at others' expense

is the treachery of consciousness. Each sheltering embrace is paid for with the greasy handshake of family investments.

You step carefully over cables and tools. Remember other schedules walking. Remember that the dry season coincides with the sex tourism season here, dumb brown trash pouring in from the hills to keep their families alive during the drought. In the nineteenth century, prostitution expanded after the British pressured Thailand to grow rice for export. The small upcountry farmers had always grown rice, even in the most unpredictable of moments. But now there was a new hunger to feed. A new tempest to weather. It wasn't so much the crops that changed. It was the language. Subsistence became poverty, greed became ambition. Your great-grandparents became a resource. They learned to understand their bodies as prospects, dependent on an unquenchable commerce, dominated by foreign desires. Desires that never reach the limits of necessity. Last month Luk finished construction of a new resort up north, far away from the city's urbane deposits of light. The land the hotel is built on used to belong to three families who never had the proper rights to it anyway. Luk doesn't know where they are now, somewhere in the currents of global resettlement. Perhaps you can trace your origins to this tide: promiscuous migrants crossing rivers of piss and concrete, imported to form an impotent working class. A class outside. A class with no stakes in the land they worked. And only now do newspaper editorials dare to ask, against the threat of lèse-majesté, Who benefits from a nation's development? If people no longer grow rice, they need to buy it. Somebody has to go out and get a job in the new ascendant economy. In the country, the one remnant of the matriarchal civilizations that predated nationhood is that the daughter is still responsible for the family. In some northern villages, up to 70 percent of girls over the age of eleven work in the sex industry to support their families. A government minister says it's because modernity has deteriorated traditional values. The parents of these children, he says, want to buy cars, TVs, refrigerators. The full truth runs deeper, more obscene. The colonies are not just a source of raw material. They're a market-place as well. Something you heard from a drunk Australian tourist falling off his bar stool: *This country is a pretty bitch, and pretty bitches tend to get raped.*

But you. You were not born pretty or a bitch. The man in the moving toilet said it best. You are a piece of work. You have never lived anywhere near true arrogance, true rapture. Unseen vines tie you close to the equator, a place where the canals are thick with relentless history and garbage. Your rich boyfriends indulged you in all the polished crevices of Europe and North America, but the vines always drag you back here. This place where rape is considered a price to pay so that 5 percent of the global population can gorge themselves on half the wealth gener-ated by the entire world.

Even as the plane touched down, you knew you were doomed to play the same games forever. Even as the plane touched down, you knew you were doomed to pay the same bribes forever. Luk says the only thing that Thai people can't stand is to eat alone. To starve with the same loneliness people have suffered since the arrival of the first European. But people are trained to accept that kind of starvation as natural. The turn of phrase that's most popular these days in the city's riskier bars is *I'm afraid to do without more than I'm afraid of AIDS.* To do without. Was there life before the body became an equation? One U.S. dollar equals. Your poverty has always fed the First World. But have you ever talked to the generals who run this show? No, no. This is not the Third World. They'll tell you without the faintest sarcasm, This is the First

World. They'll show you the parts of the narrative that say we've never been mastered.

In another city. In another place. Luk would have had to submit his plans for approval. Months would have been lost. Waiting. The Ministry in Charge. Public safety and all that. But the law is for people who don't know each other. We're all family here.

There is a *bo* tree in the forest proclaiming the *dhamma*. That *bo* tree is announcing its emptiness, something that it shares with all things, but people don't hear its proclamation. How could they? Let me ask you this. I know you're concerned about our growth. But if a tree falls in a forest. If a tree falls in a forest and there's no TV cameras around. If a tree falls in a forest of same trees, who profits from the timber?

A Thai real estate developer is building a mini-town for gay men that will feature everything from theaters to tennis courts. The project manager told the press, "Gay men need a place to live where they can feel comfortable and accepted." The town is called Flowertown and is located in the northeast, in the same province as Luk's hotel, the same rural province where the average household income is 4200 baht a year. An ad says the resort will have "handsome and charming" male staff to bring "excitement or entertainment to your room, everything and everywhere." Half of the units have been sold already, only a few of them to foreigners.

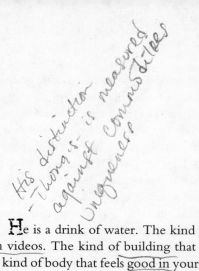

His distinction —
Thanghis — is measured
against commodities
impulses?

He is a drink of water. The kind of body you don't see in
porn videos. The kind of building that is no longer being built.
The kind of body that feels good in your hand. Like a loaded gun.
Powerful. Hard to imagine.

Oh, the money thing. Look at me. I may have left the game
this year, but do I really look like I need to pay somebody?

What do little boys do on dates in the tropics? Go and see a
movie. I think I'm breaking rules, taking a prostitute on a date
during the day. I'm not talking about just taking him out to a bar
and buying him drinks to loosen him up. This is different. I'm
transgressing roles, crossing borders, that kind of thing.

Of course I pay for his ticket.

The movie is *Batman*. Don't be disappointed. There's not
much else to see here. When we line up for tickets in the afternoon I'm suddenly aware of the mass of my own body, leaning
against my bones. My gestures reveal hidden threats. Last night I
wouldn't think twice about holding him, but in the middle of the
crowd I can't bring my hands out of my pockets. I see men touch-

ing other men here all the time. I see women walking together hand in hand, but I don't know what the union of our particular limbs means. I don't hear how Thong describes it when he runs into a girl from his school on line. She lowers her head in greeting and I smile, but it is the wrong smile. More a grimace than a smile. The same deference I greedily embrace at night makes the inside of my throat dry with terror today, when all I want is solidarity. Before the lights go down, the national anthem goes off and the theater stands in unified silence. It's only by the last stanzas that I can understand what's being sung.

> *They shall allow no one*
> *To rob them of their independence.*
> *Nor shall they suffer tyranny.*
> *All Thais are ready to give up*
> *Every drop of blood for the nation's*
> *Safety, freedom, and progress.*

Then the lights flicker shut and another myth unfolds.

> —*You ever see a Rolls get chopped? Uncle Tito asks me.*
>
> *I am eleven years old. Ba has taken me to the place where he works, Uncle Ong's garage. Uncle Tito rubs my neck and pushes me forward to see the cars get taken apart. It's a beautiful thing to watch. The roar of torches and saws echoes in the small garage. Sparks coat the floors. Ba is in his mechanic's uniform, sloppy with oil. His skin looks so impervious. As if nothing could hurt him. Ever. He and the other mechanics are crowded around a Silver Shadow suspended above the shop floor. Its gray flesh seems dulled, its sparkle dissolved in a dim bath of light from a spare bulb and the shop's one greasy window. Rolls-Royce. Symbol of power. Silver*

Shadow. Silver Ghost. There is a flash of torch on the far end of the Rolls, and then the bottom falls out with a great thud. The cylinders remain perfectly taut. Only the tires bounce.

The flayed skin of the Rolls swings over the engine. Skin that exists only to caress. The fine layer of grease coating the faces of the mechanics does not disguise their joy or lust. And me? I'm embarrassed to admit it, but I'm struck by the same feelings as my father and his co-workers. In this picture, my eyes are wide, my feet unable to move. A layer of bliss spreads slowly over my own skin, a thin layer of something that threatens to incinerate me at any moment.

The engine beckons. Its cylinders shine perfectly. These same engines that propel men into flight. That carry flesh as thoughtlessly as napalm. These workhorses that somehow epitomize luxury, fractured. The pieces of seduction. Polished and warm, each organ, each setting, each cylinder calls to me. Like beginnings without ends.

The mechanics converge on the carcass like hungry animals. They knowingly disassemble the machine until the only thing that remains is the wicked gleam of steel and oil. I inspect every piece as it is taken off. Needily. As if the engine itself held the secrets of my own desire. I want to see what's inside this great symbol of power and lust. I want to see what makes me burn.

In the less affluent archipelagoes that surround us, there is a lively traffic in human heads. The heads are smuggled back across the border by Teochew businessmen. They are destined for the cornerstones of new high-rises like the ones Luk designs. It is the vestige of an old and vaguely illegal custom: to inter the bodies of the lower castes under the threshold of a royal household. Traditionally, the lower castes delivered themselves willingly, in exchange for the promise of elevation, a higher social position in the next life. In the ruins of our dreams, the power of architecture is always overestimated. The good it can do. The bad it has done.

But then, a threshold is just another name for the ocean at the end of the known world. The place where time gains the upper hand over space, where relations start to matter more than mere things. Place has ceased to be of importance now that power no longer lives at a fixed address. It has shed as many of its static attachments as possible. Power's location is less important than its velocity through temporary obstacles. The speed of a tank ramming through the barricade of history. The remains lie splintered across Rajadmnoen Boulevard. In this city, there are no more stories, only the shredded remains of time. Every day we travel through its ruins. From the fetid preindustrial slums of Klong Toei to the electronic glitter of the Sogo department store. From consumer to consumed.

One morning I leave Thong to go on a tour of the city with Luk. It is easier than I thought to forget about him, if only for a few hours, and if only because I know I will see him again at the end of the day. Luk's driver inches through the afternoon congestion, taking advantage of every open space to push the gas pedal to the floor. Luk laughs from the backseat when we heave forward, then stop abruptly. We do this for a whole day, traversing the city from site to site, breathing in the handful of buildings his firm has designed as they take on physical shape. Sometime between lunch and rush hour, the traffic eases up and the driver tears down Thanon Petchaburi. The city flies by, stranded, its ozone spires suddenly humbled by our speed.

—This is our decade.

Luk says it without pausing for breath. He turns his head to look out the window, where old storefronts are sandwiched underneath new skyscrapers, bisected by the conduits of the new

city's destruction is capital's gain

superhighway. The city is burgeoning even as it falls apart. The foundation of every graceful arc is a base of pure ugliness.

—But ugly cities have great futures. There is nothing but elation in Luk's voice.

—It's contagious. If you get close enough to it, you're going to turn ugly too.

—Don't be so romantic. You know, sometimes you have to become part of the ugliness.

Luk says nothing else until we arrive at the site of a bank that an associate in his firm designed. The site is occupied by an office tower that was built only a year ago. Today, we leave the air-conditioned comfort of the car to watch it being readied for demolition. The new bank will be built once the rubble has been cleared. As we leave the car, the manager of the site salutes us and hands us dusty yellow hard hats. The warm air outside feels dangerous, working its way into our skin. I feel my armpits dampening in spite of myself, and soon a torrent of sweat pours off my back, fixing my shirt to my body. From a table strewn with oversized pages and blueprints, Luk listens to the manager describe the building's destruction. I listen to him ramble in fluent, familiar English, and when I ask him if he's ever been to the States he smiles shyly and says he grew up in Los Angeles.

In any other city on the planet's surface, the three of us can pass. Pass for the city's infrastructure. It's only our objection at being sent to the messenger room upon arrival that distinguishes *us* from *them*. It's only our insistence on what we think is dignity that marks us apart. All around, workers who bear only the most superficial resemblance to us maneuver in the dull sun. If they are sweating, it has been absorbed long ago by the dust caking their masks and clothes. They laugh and speak freely among themselves, as if we can neither hear nor understand what is being discussed.

indignation & dignity = class markers

Young Thai Americans are transnational subjects that lubricate collaborations w/ multinational capital

And the truth is, none of us can fully grasp what is being exchanged in front of us. None of us has ever learned their dialect, even though we have instinctualized our disdain for its outback Lao drawl. We know they are speaking for us when they switch to Thai. It is an awkward, unsure, and faulty Thai, but it's a language that still lives in their mouths. For us, it has hardened into a well-rehearsed parody, a near-desperate cry to append ourselves to a place that no longer exists. For us, it is a language that is as synthetic as this potential building. As synthetic as us, the "we" to whom the decade is dedicated.

—Pay attention to the buildings along the way, Luk says, as he struts like Auntie Mame, leading me back to the car. The ruins around us seem much larger now. There is almost more rubble in the city than buildings. *How can anyone live here?* I'm not sure if I said this or if I was just thinking it, but Luk reminds me. A city is not a place where people come to live. Its architecture was never about homes. Even the most superficial excavation will reveal its ancient heart began with the building of tombs.

[handwritten marginalia: "Transnational subject & language / illusory synthesis = nationalist 'we'" and "globalization's disruption of place & synthetic language = illusory"]

I see him every night that week. The security guards at the hotel never challenge him when we are together. We can pass for brothers. One night, though, a security guard stops us both by the elevator. He wants to know where we are going. He's talking down to us. Thong doesn't speak. He looks at me. I look at the guard. His face is creased with authority. Finally I say something. I say, in English, that we are cousins. That he is staying with me until we go down south to see our family. He smiles broadly and apologizes for his mistake. In English. We are laughing when the elevator doors shut him out.

English → authority

Inside Satellite, the biggest dance palace in the city. Inside the same darkness, unseen arms support me. The same rhythms and the same rituals repeated endlessly. Thon asks O for a cigarette, and even though O despises him they get down on the floor and salute each other, tucking their legs behind them, passing the cigarette over their bowed heads and reverent palms. My thumb pushes the grooved wheel of a lighter. Sparks. Flame. Smoke. The sound of the Asian dub-down nation. *Fire down in Babylon.* An angry chorus sliding off the turntables into the same emptiness. Inside the same ruling junta. The same families passing the same substances across

27

the same borders. No oceans divide our acts as we settle down at bar stools off the dance floor and order a bottle of gin and a bucket of ice. I have done this before. In other cities, other nights. So often I can repeat each gesture without owning any of them.

In my room, he collapses on the bed, high on rum and Coke, his body shaking quietly against the mattress. He cries without sobbing: Cream tears flooding across shady terraces of earth and seed.

—Until this year I went to St. John's, he says. —There were a lot of kids from St. John's at Satellite tonight. I couldn't look them in the face. I'm ashamed.

I think of something intelligent and comforting I can say to all this. In fact, there is nothing to say to all this. I respond by repeating his words, assuring him that I'm listening.

—Ashamed.

—I'm a call girl. I'm poor. I don't have a father.

—You don't have a father.

—I have a father. I have a mother. That's not the problem.

—What's the problem, Thong?

—My father doesn't love me.

I count the money in my wallet, watching him from the corner of my eye. He's not even looking. I throw the wad of bills, each one blessed with His Majesty's portrait, across the room at the mirror. He turns and frowns.

—You should know better. You should show some respect.

Some places you just don't go. Each confidence draws me closer to him. Makes me feel like I'm not just another client. I want

28

to ask him about his customers so we can laugh about them together. But whenever I bring it up, he says he doesn't understand.

He eases a silver ring on my finger at Les Beaux. Ropes of
sterling coil around my knuckle.

—Thong is very popular. But he likes you.

His manager is beaming. I roll the ring around my bony
knuckle.

The next morning:

—Here's my wallet. Just take what you need, OK? I'm never
sure if I'm giving you enough.

I'm getting tired of this charade, besides.

He doesn't take anything.

He loves me so much, he takes me home to live with him.

—We can save money this way, he says. —The hotels are
so expensive.

—But I don't care about the money. I just want to be with
you.

But he needs the money

Perfect lovers. Two identical clocks side by side ticking time
in perfect harmony.

Romantic love → Presumption of equivalence that material inequality disrupts

29

You and I took our first breath with the ashes of napalm in our mouths. The newspapers this morning carry a small news item that is probably meaningless to anyone else. Admiral Elmo Zumfalt, the man who ordered the spraying of Agent Orange across large areas of Vietnam, has returned to the country he deforested. His own son died of cancer provoked by the chemical, but Zumfalt told Thai newspapers he would drop it all again because of the American lives it saved. The admiral has returned, in the waning hours of the international embargo, to visit. One of the stops on his trip is a hospital where the children born to Vietnamese exposed to Agent Orange are housed.

Two sisters, eight and ten, appeared to put him under severe pressure. The admiral, stern and upright for most of his visit, was glancing away and gesturing to leave as a nurse displayed the smiling sisters' stunted spines and twisted limbs. Their father, the nurse told him, fought in the south and was exposed to Agent Orange. Zumfalt repeatedly avoided requests to get closer to the children, saying he "really had to leave." Ten minutes into his visit the admiral ran out of the hospital, muttering about having an urgent personal appointment.

30

He doesn't know who his father is. His mother works in a factory. He has two brothers, two sisters. They all live in a shack with a dirt floor somewhere in the slums of Klong Toei. Somewhere along the railroad tracks that bring you into the city.

The cab slides by the guard at the entrance to his *muban,* a side street in suburban Ladprao. At the edge of the *muban* my driver stops. This is it, he says. We look out the window at an electronic gate and, behind it, a long driveway that leads up to an impressive garden, and then the house itself, smooth white walls and a red-tiled roof.

His father, it turns out, is a sugar merchant. His big house is nothing like the houses I remember as a child. It is actually three times as big as the leased shack with the tin roof we left a decade ago. His grandfather comes from more modest means. He walks around the house barefoot, bare-chested, blue Khmer tattoos covering his leathery shoulders. He barely speaks, but when he opens his mouth, his words are black seraphim fleeing emptied gardens. Angels flying in a cadence so dusty and rural it shames his children.

Dinner the first night is a minor feast his stepmother has prepared. No one says whose honor it's in but I assume it's mine. We take it on the terrace overlooking the grassy lot next door. Over dinner his father tries to make conversation.

—There are snakes in there.

He points to the field he will one day buy.

—Uh-huh. Mmm. Snakes. That's great.

—You like my son.

This is not a question but knowledge he is sharing with me. To let him know I understand this, though, I answer it like a question.

—Yeah. Umm. I like your son.

—I'm glad he's going to be working with you.

Ladling rice onto my plate, Thong is quiet.

During the rainy season the basement floods, but tonight it's our room. Cool and moldy. I lock the door behind us. Thong stretches out on the bed.

—Does your father know the deal between us?

—Do you?

A rocket or a bridge. That's the only way I can really describe it. If there is a river between our sleeping bodies, this is the bridge that crosses it. If there is something besides the stinking surface of this planet, I'll only get there by clinging to it. Holding tight. Early in the morning, my head still fuzzy with last night's dream, I can just fit my fist around the base without waking him. I love it so much I want to bite it. I want to chew it up and swallow it. A trail of black alfalfa leaps up from between his legs, gets caught in my teeth. As much as I try to stuff into my mouth, there's still more, suffocating me. It tickles the back of my throat, brings something sour and hot up from my stomach. I could offer him my ass, but what's the point? It's my mouth that makes the words. It's my mouth that brings the past to life inside. The night they brought me back from the hospital a cobra crawled into the house, shed its oily fleece under my crib, and left before the sun came up. Life, death, and then life again. No, no. Something more than life itself. When I feel his bones move underneath his flesh, pull them tight against my teeth, I know I'm no longer conscious. No longer alive. That this is just the beginning of time, my whole life in front of me. My whole fall in front of me. He barely works up a sweat when he comes in my mouth, warm bursts of the ocean that melt away into light at the back of my throat.

He wants to get his ear pierced. We take a taxi all the way to Central Plaza and slip into the sprawling air-conditioned shopping complex, listlessly passing through racks of clothes, staring at electronic appliances. A woman with acne symmetrically crossing her face like red cauliflowers pierces his ear in a gift shop. I buy him an ice-cream cone at a cappuccino bar, and we sit and watch couples towing their children around. He gets all excited when he sees a kid.

—They're so cute.

He enthuses. He smirks. He wants to have a baby one day. He confides, and in that confidence his face becomes an ember, threatening with a beauty that I've never had and that no one will ever own, no matter how fat a tip they leave him. I put my hand over his, wondering if he notices.

A little girl walks up to us. He fishes in his pockets for some change to give to her. I follow suit.

—Don't you feel pity for her?

I shake my head. No way. I scrape my veins for the right words and then dive for my dictionary, because there are no words in my vocabulary for what I feel for her. I point to the word *empathy* and score the Thai word next to it with my fingernail.

I watch the girl amble into the crush of milling consumers outside the bar. Somehow, the poverty that spawned her seems even more remote than she is. We were growing, far above her tiny vanishing figure. Soon she would mean nothing. We were growing so fast and we needed a respite from people like her, from the fried locusts and crumbling sidewalks outside the mall. We needed to retreat from those reminders.

Now I know what development means: air-conditioning.

With air-conditioning, we can have civilization, which exists only in temperate climates. We can abandon the tropical streets to beggars and leave the temples in ruins. Those places are no longer safe. They're pockmarked with crime and disease. The only safety is in the private ammonia-scented corridors of the mall like this one. Here we can surrender lives that are too complex to be lived any longer. Here we can find happiness and security under the oppression of the senses.

Safety = Sterility

It's while wandering past the stands full of jewelry that you lose yourself for a moment. Shed one of your cumbersome presences. The moody one with the big head. The one that walks with the stilted pace of a boy who's been wounded on the playground. Lose it in a display case full of glittering metal and wheels of unending chain. Some the color of honey. Some the color of light. You misplace him under a square of red plastic with a promise of paradise daubed out in fading yellow ink. Gold by the inch. Thong's walking ahead of you, but returns when he sees you leaning respectfully over a box of gold rings.

Gold by the inch = fool's gold

I buy him one and put it on his finger.

presumption of equivalence

35

There are mostly noisy, wordless exchanges in shopping malls, averted glances on escalators. Sometimes I can't bring myself to look at him, how young and perfect he is. We talk in sentences only to the point where we misplace a phrase, a term, an idiom. Then one of us will open the thick dictionary with the green plastic cover and underline a word with a fingernail. He's fluent in a language I learned only as chastisement or in the breathing of confidences. But there is always his voice, stripped and serious, or teasing, more than anything we ever say. I love the way he talks so much that I often forget what he's saying. I love the way he talks Thai. Rough. Surly. Impatient. Like he owns it.

Ownership = basis o' admiration + pleasure

—*Why are you doing this? Is it the money?*
—*No, it's not the money. But, yeah, it's that too.*

I'm enjoying our relationship at the moment because it feels like I'm living off him. *How parasitical*

You were sleeping when I finished washing up and closed the door to our room. You were sleeping naked, an even gold slash in the white sheets, your penis lying dormant like an ear or a nautilus between your legs. I was suddenly overcome with fear as I realized you, whom I'd thought my twin, were nothing like me. Our difference seemed so wide in that moment, something that would never be bridged. You would never love anyone, anything, as much as I loved you now. I fell back into the bed, too scared to hold you but too tired, or high, to care. The cool sheets reached up around my sides. I felt my body dissolve into a million tiny ants, and as I hoped they would climb inside your head, devour your dreams, and bring them back to me, they defied me, growing wings and scattering across the million different points of the compass.

He realizes that equivalence suggested by romance is all an illusion

"*The man who owned these slaves behaved like a beast, shameless and without fear of Allah. The younger girls hung round him while he behaved in a manner which it would be improper for me to describe in this book. For anyone who wished to buy these slave-girls he would open their clothing with all manner of gestures of which I am ashamed to write. The slave dealers behaved in the most savage manner, devoid of any spark of feeling, for I noticed that when the little children of the slaves cried they kicked them head over heels and struck their mothers with a cane, raising ugly weals on their bodies. To the young girls, who were in great demand, they gave a piece of cloth to wear, but they paid no attention to the aged and the sick. The greatest iniquity of all that I noticed was the selling of a woman to one man and of her child to another. The mother wept and the child screamed and screamed when she saw her mother being taken away. My feelings were so outraged by this scene that, had I been some-one in authority, I would most certainly have punished the wicked man responsible for it. Furthermore, those in charge of male slaves tied them round the waist like monkeys, one to each rope, made fast to the side of the boat. They relieved nature where they stood and the smell on the boat made one hold one's nose.*"*

—Abdullah bin Abdul Kadir Munshi
on the slave market in Singapore,
Hikayat Abdullah

Retak Menanti Pechah:
The Crack Awaiting
the Break

OK, OK. You're writing a postcard on a ferry, crossing the North Channel. You could tell us you're Duras pining for Sadec or Suzie Wong leaving Kowloon, or even Marlow cruising the Congo, but in the end you're just a big-headed bitch on a boat. There is no wind. There were no welcoming kisses. You must have been dreaming. It hurts to remember all this, an interim of embarrassment and clumsiness. But in the end, it's your favorite memory.

In the late afternoon you make the crossing clutching a sheaf of postcards, an accordion that extends down half your body. "Historic Buildings of George Town, Penang."

The picture on the front of the postcard.

Your father forbade you to know about your grandmother. She died of starvation during the Japanese occupation. You came back to Penang to find pictures of her. In those days, Auntie says, nobody had time for snapshots. You imagine her, a shard of smoke carried on fetid trade winds. Her hair is pulled back over a high forehead; light face, with two smudges for eyes. Two tiny gold swastikas are pinned to her earlobes. She is wearing a blue floral print smock and wide black trousers. She is a name on a tombstone, a name that never made the middle passage. Mme. Le Arn Sayneevongse, aka Mrs. Khoo Siew Hin: a story your father will never tell. A story you will have to make yourself.

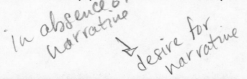

43

The writing on the back. The stamp in the corner.

Your ancestors believed the camera had a different power over their lives. If your picture was taken more than three times, you would die.

You write three postcards on the trip across the channel, and when you get to the other side you tear all of them up and watch the small pieces of cardboard drift off into the sea as people on the dock look on disapprovingly.

Another day. Another country. An hour on the plane. A day on the train. You've left all your shit up in Bangkok. Your plan is to stay sober for one month here, where the penalty for possession is death. Uncle, the construction worker, wants to know why Luk didn't come down to visit with you.

—Too busy *lah*. Always building.

You've left Thong there too. You didn't know how to explain him to your family. The separation will be good, you tell him. *I'm getting too attached to you.* And then you say, knowing you will regret it the minute the words are past your lips, *I think I'm falling in love with you.*

Tonight is your first night back in Penang in thirteen years. You are lying in your cousins' room in the back. They are next door, sleeping three on a mattress. Uncle gave you this room because it has an air conditioner, but you won't turn it on. Not tonight. It's been so long since you slept like this, in the heat. The warm air holds you, won't let you fall. A lover's embrace. Outside the window, a congress of barking dogs tries to keep you awake. But nothing will keep you from your dreams tonight. You want to dream of your father's death. Not his corpse, bloated and depressing, but the lightness of having his life finally severed from yours. His body is several thousand miles away now, but not far enough.

—What's he eating?

Auntie is peering around the wall separating the kitchen from the dining room table. When you woke up late this morning, she stopped scouring the breakfast dishes and poured you a cup of coffee, thick as crude petrol. Now you're folding a slice of whole wheat bread around a finger-sized banana, pretending you can't understand what she's saying.

—*Roti.*

Your cousin Martina tells her. You can't eat enough to please Auntie. But she won't let you near the cooking. One afternoon when everyone else is out of the house she will give in and show you how to pit and slice a mango. You will take this trick around with you, acting like you always knew how.

Is this dirt or soil you're supposed to kiss when you step down from the plane? Always the return. Going back. The scenes are the same. An unchanged unmoving street with the same greasy food vendors the same dripping palms the same monkey chained to the same spot on the same impossibly green lawn. Always the same litany of smells, tastes, feelings. The same recipes handed down from generation to generation. When you go home. And then the list of fragile specialties no one can import. The same. Nothing is the same. Nothing is the way you remember it.

Your cousin Ah Meng is lying in his room at the front of the house, with its sliding gate for a door. He's lying on his bed, staring at the ceiling, his tiny Japanese stereo turned up full blast. The mighty poet Dub Roy is on the wire, saxophone dripping like treacle. Ah Meng mumbles along, mangling the lyrics:

Tit for tat and butter for fish.
Call me anything you wish it's the same dish.
Tit for tat and butter for fish.
Down in Penang we eat nasi lemak *and salt fish.*

Somewhere better than this place.

Nowhere better than this place.

Morning. On the Esplanade. Staring at the ocean, the waves leaving you behind, lazy. The smell of crabs crawling over the jetty. Knowing you're never going anywhere.

Auntie is showing you the frayed snapshots your mother used to send. They came to her in bundles every month for the first few years. Then they stopped suddenly. You were a family of four when you left. Your grandfather died clutching your photograph.

You know the image that saw him expire. In it, you are standing at the edge of the forest behind the house, mouth wide open and anguished, eyes squeezing tears. Your grandfather will gamble away the house soon after the photo is taken. He will die bitter and angry in Uncle's back room in Tanjong Tokong while you are being handcuffed around the tank of a public toilet on the other side of the world.

—Auntie, is it true you can tell from a picture of someone if they're alive or not?

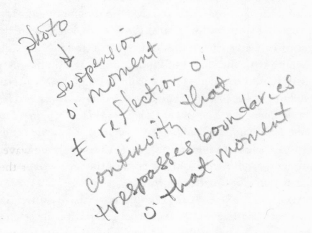

An Organized Practical
Understanding of the
True Nature of Things,
or What Is What

Tabula rasa. Start from there: a clean slate. Rebuild the home from scratch. It's not Uncle but the muezzin who welcomes me back to ground zero on the first morning back in Penang. The announcement comes from the minaret on the television in Uncle's living room just as the sun rises and my cousins get ready for school and the factory. Uncle has been up for an hour already, ready to report to his building site. Only I am left out of the morning rituals. Only I have the luxury to sit and listen to the *azhan* compete with the sound of Uncle coughing up phlegm in the sink. Last night's tobacco. This morning's religion. *The expression of real distress. The protest of real distress. Allah yang maha besar. The sigh of the oppressed. The soul of a soulless world. The spirit of social conditions from which any spirit has been excluded. The opium of the masses.* The call fades into the morning news: a story about Khmer Rouge orphans, twelve-year-old children of the Year Zero who killed their parents for a better world.

Growing up in New York, I would never have known Ba had parents. He would never talk about them. Occasionally, a letter would arrive from home, written in someone else's hand because no one back here could read or write. History drifted from these impossibly thin sheets of paper to become abstract traces on concrete walls, eventually overwritten by a stronger hand. A few days before my first Christmas in New York, Ba took me to a Roman Catholic church down the street. After he taught me to kiss my hand when I had finished crossing myself, we stood there in the pews for a second, looking at the empty building. Then, suddenly, Ba seized my hand, the one I had just kissed, and we left to go shopping. We arrived in quiet awe at a store two city blocks long, thronged with customers and goods. Swirling plastic race cars. Bicycles. Fishing gear. What I really wanted was a dog but I settled for a race car set with cars that fly across the floor. Ba pulled a red PAID sticker from his pocket and slapped it on the box.

—Don't tell your mother.

His grip tightened around my hand. His eyes lit me up with terror. I wanted to cry, but instead we walked out the front entrance; my ten-year-old heart missed one full beat passing the security guard. I was confused, but Ba wasn't. He walked out of that store like those goodies we stole belonged to him.

Only a few years after that, Ba left Ma and then left New York. He bounced around from city to city, deeper into obscurity. He remarried—an American woman—and then finally settled for a few years in Los Angeles. I saw him there, broken, and encouraged him to move back home. He took my advice, returning to his birthplace to terrorize his remaining family. Then, finally, he took his last residence in Honolulu. I couldn't bring myself to visit. Waited five years until I heard he was dying. That made me feel better, knowing the act wouldn't have to be repeated. But it wasn't his pending death that was so unnerving. It was his life. The dirt and the jetsam crammed into the tiny apartment he shared with his new wife behind the shopping center. How many useless gadgets, appliances, and unnecessary furnishings shadowed the small space.

Shadowed him.

Television sets. Food processors. Commemorative plates for the lunar landing and the Challenger disaster. Tote bags ordered from the sides of cigarette cartons. Cheap costume jewelry and worthless watches. Certificates Luk and I won as children (mostly Luk). Honor roll. Luk's diploma from high school. Ba clutched his memories in objects. An endless parade of stray cats wandered aimlessly in and out of his apartment. There was a large crucifix hanging on the wall, above the portraits of my great-grandparents he had stolen from Uncle's house in Penang. But a carpet on the floor, moldy and caked with insect limbs and filth, repelled me more. When I tried to persuade him to get rid of it, he became incensed.

—I'm not happy with the way you are living your life.

I ignored him until he repeated himself. Then I spoke.

—That's fine. I'm not happy with the way you live yours.

—There is no life for me, he said. —Only death.

I laughed. It was a slow, unsteady laugh that did not alter Ba's features.

—You know what your problem is? He didn't wait for me to answer. —Your problem is you don't believe in anything.

The dream of the starving is to be fed. The dream of the children of the starving is to have appliances. He was dwarfed by the acquisitions in his apartment. Defeated. His ashen skin hidden by a baseball cap. Chain-smoking Kools. No color. No blood. No life. He lived long enough to complain about the Filipino who tried to take away his night shift at work. Ba had been working all his life toward a goal he could no longer describe. I stood there in the doorway, wanting to flee. Not listening to his words. Wondering at this man who used to terrify me. Who used to beat me when I wouldn't clean my plate. Who called me spoiled when I left over a grain of rice. Wondered at how this small, lifeless man

commodities
↓
(supposedly)
memory
+∆
Stop Bas
longing to be
remembered

GOLD BY THE INCH

could have ever intimidated me. I almost missed the terror. I
watched his body sleeping on the floor early in the morning. The
body of my father. Broken. Pained. Aching to be remembered.

Morning market. Taman Fettes. Everyone is here. I can trace
every member of my calabash family here. Auntie running the
kedai kopi, where I order my coffee *o kosong* and get a cup of frothy
unsweetened pitch. Uncle Ah Seng pressing a few extra *buah cikgu*
in my hands when I tell him how long it's been since that fruit
has crossed my lips. My cousin bringing a copy of the *Star* to read
over breakfast. They all know me before I introduce myself: the
son come back. I go to pay respects to uncle Ah Sem. A squat
dun man standing at a soup cart cutting squiggly *kway teow* from
a nearly translucent white block. He barely looks up when I say
his name. He sighs.

—Uncle told you about the trouble your father—
Before he can continue he looks up and sees my face. Stops.
—Yeah, yeah, he told me all about it.

Ba came back here after losing his job in Los Angeles, his
savings, and his right to residence in America. He came back with
a ticket Luk bought him. Within a month, my cousins were writing short, urgent letters for their parents, begging us to come take
him back to America. *We have known no peace since he came,* they
wrote. When Ba arrived, he looked for the house I was born in, a
house built on land leased by the Catholic Church. But it had been
reclaimed to build a seminary. The church—the Sacred Heart of
Jesus Limited—gave Uncle a small fee to resettle. Ba claimed
Uncle's new house as his own, his due as the family's eldest son,
regardless of his absence. When Uncle smiled ambivalently instead
of acknowledging Ba's claim, Ba tried to burn down the house.

Now I cannot bring myself to tell them. He is dead.

Was it his rage he finally choked on? His body looked as if it had burned from within. Scalded white. I marveled at its collapse.

Uncle insists Ba's actions have no bearing on me. We can make a family without him, he says. I feel secure hearing that. But still, I half wonder if this reconstituted family expects me to be the proof of the better life he made for himself. They observe me. Smile at my awkwardness, my stumbling through the language. As if they are looking at something inhabited by more than one self. More and less than one. Me and you. In the mess but not of it.

I died when I was ten and that's when you were born. Confused. Hungry. Nostalgic. Crying for attention. That's how you came into the world when the plane took off, circled Subang International Airport, and then tore off into the clouds. There was no airport in Penang then. My great-grandmother and some aunties took the overnight train with us through the forest to Kuala Lumpur. We arrived bleary-eyed and confused. I spent an hour or two sleeping in my brother's lap, before waking up to the call of the muezzin bouncing off the railway station's roof. A big Peugeot taxi carried us to the airport. I cannot remember the rituals at the airport, or the waiting, not even the goodbyes, the formality, and then the tears, mostly from the family that wasn't leaving. I remember my great-grandmother, sticking a bag of oranges or mangosteens in my hand before we left.

—Listen, don't be arrogant there. Be humble, because we are humble people. Remember us here back in the . . .

Or perhaps she didn't say anything.

Just smiled weakly as we left her behind.

I was too bewildered to feel anything but excitement and then, perhaps, relief as I boarded the plane, forgetfully leaving the bag of red fruit in the airport. Yes. I remember feeling relief as we climbed the steps to the plane, not looking behind me, feeling my great-grandmother's eyes on my shoulders. Feeling as if a burden had been lifted from me as I receded into the depth of the plane. But still too young to know what that burden was.

Why doesn't author tell us what burden is?

Dark Shore
Just Seen
It Was Rich

There is no meaning at the end of the superhighway. Its surfaces, conceited as skin, lead effortlessly down the trail of an impossible and terrifying final reality. The signs along the edge all point to its imminent collapse. Signs more often than not whispered in splinters of postcoital anxiety. Signs so beguiling as to seem seductive. Signs as familiar as the pillows worn to clouds by our bodies. Signs like:

—Why do you love me?

I wasn't sure I heard it the first time Jim said it. I asked him to repeat it, to be sure there was no mistaking the question. He repeated slowly, taking care to shape his mouth precisely around each syllable:

—Why do you love me?

In the moment after he spoke, I became suddenly aware of my hand resting on his side, of the impossible way our bodies were contorted, and of how we could lie to ourselves that this position was comfortable.

—I love you—

I began, stopped. Started all over.

—I love you because you love me.

An alliance crumbles in layers. False name. False history. False life. The first layer consists of what we had in common. We were

1st layer =
crumbling
alliance

the same age. Is that enough to establish the beginnings of a friend-ship? A relationship? Love? Whatever. Jim was an interior designer. Luk introduced us. Jim wasn't handsome or bright, but he was well paid and he had a profound sense of decoration. He was al-ways surrounding himself with things he considered "beautiful." The coke he funneled up his sinuses merely heightened his ap-preciation of that beauty. Jim's voice had assumed the soft, nasal twang of Winnie the Pooh after having his nose reconstructed twice. A nose that slid down narrow between gray eyes and tight, pale skin. Skin as unconcerned as it was unapproachable.

I noticed how different we looked one morning, standing to-gether in front of the bathroom mirror, his arms draped around me.

—You look like an angel.

I looked again.

—And I look like the devil.

It is not good for a person to look like an angel. It fucks with his character.

The second layer is about equity. Depending on how the word is used, it can mean cash value or justice. Anyone observ-ing us from a distance might believe there was a certain amount of both involved in being his decorative companion. If nothing else, and I know this sounds mercenary, I got a lot of free plane tickets out of it. He was constantly trawling for antiques: Florence, Tokyo, Prague. On our first-month anniversary, he handed me a plane ticket to Paris. It was, he said, his favorite place. The Radiant City. We stayed in our hotel room for most of the week-end, finishing off the two grams of cocaine he had brought in his jacket pocket. (*They never check there, they always search the suit-cases,* he said, and insisted that we walk through customs as if we didn't know each other.) Once I ventured out alone while he was sleeping. I think it was probably the only time he slept

2nd layer: equity

55

during that trip. He was lying easy in the milky light of our pension, crumpled around a pillow when I left, his eyes shut in grateful repose.

It had been a long time since I had walked anywhere so consciously alone. It was the end of spring, and the warm night air teased the slimy coating of complacence that had settled on my skin. I wandered down the city's open boulevards, passing as close to other pedestrians as I could without knocking them over. I felt them brush against me. Touch my new skin. Inhaled the violence left in their wake as they passed. I wandered, with the barest direction in mind, toward Les Halles. It was my first time in this blue city, but each street and monument fell into my view with familiar precision. I felt strangely at home here, amid the trophies of civilization. At first I thought I was in the midst of someone else's civilization. I couldn't easily be called Thai or Chinese or Malaysian or American, but I certainly wasn't French. Still, every edifice and corner announced it was mine. My shoulders fell back and my legs took the lead. I ventured into the Metro with what could loosely be termed pride.

It was the wrong fare. Even before I had walked through the turnstiles, I was surrounded by ten men in black paramilitary uniforms who threw me violently against a wall and put their hands all over me. Without explanation, one held the back of my neck, quietly pressing my forehead against the wall. I felt the cool of the tile against my head, then, his hand starting to warm against me. I became aware of my skin under his grip, prickling with frustrated heat. I felt the policeman look down the collar of my shirt, felt him exhale on my back. Against his breath, my skin became a decaying act of resistance, a virus marking me as an illness. Something to contain. Something to cherish. He fished my passport out of my pocket and laughed softly in my ear.

—*Américain?*

His colleagues seemed amused and unimpressed. They brushed off my shoulders. Patted me on the back.

—*Vous êtes très gentil, monsieur.*

I didn't turn to see if their faces read smug when they said that. I went on my way.

When I told Jim what had happened, he didn't believe me. He was certain I had made up the story just to amuse him.

—Things like that never happen when we are together.

He snickered and promptly forgot the incident. I knew from then on what purpose Jim served in my life. Jim gave me the appearance of belonging: to a place, to a time, to him. As decoration, I wasn't always able to articulate my value, but Jim knew it intrinsically.

In those days, I was almost obsessed with my value. If I could have asked strangers what they thought it was without sounding indelicate, I would have. I had just started school and was studying economics. I made it through the first year and then dropped out. I remember getting through Adam Smith's *The Wealth of Nations* but really wanting to read his *Theory of Moral Sentiments*. Economists explain how production takes place in relations between classes of people. But they never explain how those relationships evolve in the first place. The Holy Qur'an says no man should bear the burden of another. Man can have only what he strives for. Maybe it is as simple as that: Don't write checks with your mouth that your ass can't cash. But I was never really a prostitute. No. I would never count the money left on top of my clothes. I was more of a worthy companion, someone who knew the prices and the categories had already been fixed. Someone who couldn't be bothered to haggle over spare change.

The third layer is that a relationship between people is exclusively a thing. Ours took on a ghoulish objectivity. It acquired a rational and all-embracing patina of autonomy that concealed its nature: a relation between people, a hectic frequency across differences, an exchange of capital and services. The thing it became was an investment, and I was frustrated when I came to collect. The dividends were getting smaller. Maturity seemed further away than ever before. It was depressing, watching all that money squandered up Jim's nose. I threatened to leave him. He promised to clean up. I believed him, and believing him meant putting it out of my mind.

In the meantime, his addiction bloomed.

We were out at a club one night, and I saw him go off into a bathroom stall with a drug dealer we had both fucked once. I could tell what he was going to do the minute I saw him disappear behind that door. I was waiting for him when he came out. He looked surprised to see me.

—You have something under your nose.

I don't know if I sounded calm when I said that. Probably not. Probably my voice was shaking. I'm not sure if I was angrier that he had broken another promise to me or that he hadn't offered to share his candy with me. Probably the latter. He rubbed the frosting off nervously. Then he slapped me. It was the first time a man other than my father had hit me. I watched him run out of the club before I could even feel the blood rising to my cheek. When I got back to our apartment that night, my clothes were all over the street, hanging off the building. I saw a woman pick up a shirt he had bought me, hold it up, and then drop it back on the sidewalk, like it was too heavy or ugly to carry away. I yelled up at our window, twenty-three stories above the street.

When I opened the door to the apartment, he was sleeping in bed. I sat there in the dark for a short time, breathing heavily, wondering what I should do now. Wondering where I could go. He finally woke up. I told him I was leaving. Had enough. He kept on saying how he didn't want me to go. I said nothing. He took my silence for an argument and became enraged. Turned. Said he wanted me out. He picked up the telephone and smashed it against my face. I felt its cold thickness disappear into a warm bath. Looked down to see blood all over the place. Knew it was my blood because it was red.

The police came. He told them I was trespassing. That they should arrest me. I begged them to let me call our next-door neighbor, who could vouch for my identity. One of them started to giggle when he put the handcuffs on me. I couldn't blame him.

I spent the night in jail. A cell about the size of my bedroom, it was built out of white cinder block smudged with the memorials of previous residents. That cinder block stuck a long time in my head. I knew right away where I had seen it before. It was the same bulwark of cement that contained us the first years I lived here with my parents and Luk in municipal housing projects. Some crazy fool had written, in ink still fresh on their fingers from the print pad, *I don't belong here*. It made me laugh. I knew better. I knew the absence between home and prison. That everything in the cell had been made specifically for it. Specifically. Including me. It's those vines. They always bring you back to the forest.

I fell asleep for fifteen minutes on that familiar concrete. Woke up with my dick hard and my body knotted over with pain. I tried washing the night's grease off in the cell's small steel sink, but there was no soap. I stood with my face by the faucet, scratching oily pieces of flesh into the basin, listening to the drain

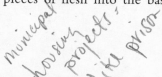

59

beneath me gulping in satisfaction. For breakfast, they fed me a tasteless ham and American cheese sandwich on soggy Wonder bread. They also fed me an apple that was already turning brown and I remember biting into it, thinking how sweet and worthless it was.

Jim finally came to the station to dismiss charges against me. He had thought it over and realized it wasn't worth it. The police returned the contents of my pockets. They had scrupulously catalogued it all, right down to the denominations of bills and coins. $24.52. Jim was there when they released me. He looked me over hard. His eyes breathing me. Appraising me. Fixing value like he always did. Like it was his job. But it was value I now knew was less than the worth of my skin. Skin the color of decay. Another layer crumbling in the rinse.

Jim holds narrator under white gaze that evaluates him as commodity

Interesting we're never told Jim is white but know it

An Inquiry Into
Our Ideas of the
Sublime and Beautiful
(Architecture of Desire)

Cities have their own way of talking to you. I admire Luk
and the way he can be impassioned, made breathless, by the arc
of a ceiling. I have to force myself to react to language in that way
sometimes. For me, the city is a stutter, its mottled, nearly suffo-
cated legacies illuminated only by tense threads of light. The city
is capital accumulated until it becomes an image. Barely. Its buildings are thin plaster shells, facades that work like the surfaces of a
photograph, locking memory in an embrace. Containing it. Stem-
ming its flood.

I made the crossing here with a sheaf of postcards: "Historic Buildings of George Town, Penang." A string of photographs, reordered buildings and stories, that became windows
onto a river of lust. I showed Auntie the postcards, and she stud-
ied them seriously. Now she wants to show me the city in the
postcards. A few nights before Christmas, we set out from the
hills behind Tanjong Tokong for George Town. The city is also
celebrating its two hundredth anniversary, the year Captain
Francis Light founded Penang. But the fishermen who found
him two hundred years ago on the beach at Tanjong Tokong
would dispute this. There were settlements here long before
Light showed up, but they did not become the gateway to
European conquest of the peninsula until a British nobleman

washed up on that beach. It was Captain Light who opened the region up to the opium trade and then the exploitation of its resources.

There is a temple here that predates the good captain's arrival. The Sea Pearl Temple is dedicated to Tua Pek Kong: the "Great-Granduncle," the "Protector of the Land," the "God of Prosperity." Many Chinese settlements in the region have their own Tua Pek Kong. Penang's is Chang Li, a Hakka scholar, exiled from eighteenth-century China. He came with two brothers, a brickmaker and a metalsmith. One could teach, one could build houses, one could make weapons. All the necessities for developing a new society. The written word. The crumbling building. The smoking gun.

Auntie picks up a bundle of joss sticks from the bin by the entrance to the temple. She lights them at the lamp in the front. I know she is saying a prayer. But that's not what I hear.

—*What is history? Is it truth? No, no . . . I think history is desire.*

I mimic her steps, keeping watch on her movements from the corner of my eye. When I think I have it down, I close my eyes. Wave the burning joss over my head. Flutter my eyelids self-consciously. Crack them open as I move forward to place them in the urn, already overflowing with incense. An attendant comes by every few minutes, picking up the burning joss sticks and throwing them into a bucket of sand.

Actually, history is nothing more than the skyline of George Town. Night is falling on it when the bus turns the road near Gurney Drive. Shadows, shifting lines that reach up to a sweating moon, then fall again on reddened roof tiles. A giant billboard of

Commodification → violation of body [handwritten annotation]

Santa Claus hangs over the food stands at Gurney Drive: pink man in a red fur coat in the emerald tropics. The shopping malls behind the city are jammed. Their aisles are packed solid. Night traffic circles impatiently by the entrance of the McDonald's at the near edge of the Esplanade. There are three full-grown men outside, dressed in life-size costumes: a hamburger, a soft drink, and a box of fries. Silent but animated, they wave to passersby. Children point and cry. Inside, the angry fluorescent lights illuminate scenes of immaculate debauchery. Whole families devour greasy hamburger patties, air-filled pockets of bread, french fries. The smell calls to you. What was life like before the body became merchandise? Free with the purchase of a medium-size soft drink, fries, and a Big Mac. Free with the purchase of a Happy Meal.

Auntie feels it's her responsibility to show me around George Town. Even though I was born here. Even though I probably know the buildings better than she does. At least she is not inquisitive about my presence here. The other night, one of my cousins took me for a drive and asked me why I came to visit Penang. As if I were some fucking tourist.

The number 94 bus, run by the Hin Bus Company, costs 70 sen from Tanjong Tokong to the Kompleks Tun Abdul Razak, better known as Komtar. The bus stops directly in front of Uncle's house, off the main road, and begins to circle back underneath the Yaohan department store windows of the center. It begins its straightforward route in the north housing projects of Telok Bahang, follows the main road through Batu Ferringhi, Tanjong

Bungah, Tanjong Tokong, Pulau Tikus, and Bagan Jermal, through the cluttered heart of George Town, into Komtar, and then finally to the jetty, where the ferry launches to the mainland.

The woman selling tickets on the bus barely says anything to her customers. She rattles her cylindrical change box at passengers. We pass over coins or bills and mumble our destination. She hands back our change. The veteran commuters are recognized immediately and passed back their change before they can say where they're going. If you give her a destination other than the eight areas listed on the front of the ticket, her face will crease with confusion.

—*Pergi ke mana?*

She says it in Malay. Auntie hesitates. There are so many places she wants to point out to me. The ticket seller gets impatient.

—You can't just sit on a bus *lah. You have to have a destination.*

Auntie could name the monuments, the buildings, the ornamentation crossing decaying verandas. But the ticket seller does not want to hear the sights along the way. She wants to know the destination. She does not want to know what monuments have been left on the sides of the journey. She wants to hear what keeps the rest of the bus going. The promise that you will actually get somewhere in the end.

Luk was right to remind me to pay attention to the architecture here. From the windows of the moving bus, the city becomes something else. Its stilled buildings become conflicting fragments. Ready-framed views are cut out of its flesh, then set up and juxtaposed against each other. Electronic surfaces, sources of light, slice against reflections, shades and shadows. Wounded cicadas stumbling through the open drains. A woman bathing her child in a plastic basin at the side of the road. A schoolboy doing his homework at the back table of his father's *nasi campur* stand. His classmates racing along the lip of the road, their schoolbags bouncing on their backs. Hands shaking at night on the Esplanade. Skin rustling. Fingers snapping under the palm trees. The traffic sticking to the bones of the city. *Penang have so many cars, ho.* A boy with strong hands leading another boy through a tiny white door, up a narrow stairway. Buy one free one. The city becomes a montage of attractions. At every junction, the buildings pull one another toward them. Where they clash becomes a river, a rippling surface where my own reflection intervenes. The story contained in each building falls away into a flood of articulate energy. Difference. Equivalence. Repetition. Conflict. Something more than dialogue. The buildings are swept away in the torrent of living context. The information once held frozen behind their walls tumbles out. Facades become language. A language so smooth it could fool you into thinking the city loved you.

—Every building on this island has a story, you know.

Auntie reminds me of this as we step off the bus and begin our tour. A story of immigration. A story of love, yes, but swathed in greed.

There is a story like that in the courtyard of a mansion on Leith Street. Built around a red, gold, and turquoise courtyard, in classic southern Chinese style, its seven staircases also incorporate distinctly European motifs like stained glass, fake wooden facades, and decorative ceiling moldings. Victorian cast iron and Chinese latticework entwine across the central courtyard's balcony. The best of both worlds. There are two photos of the owner, Cheong Fatt Tze, in the main room off the courtyard. In one, he is wearing a top hat and suit. In another he is wearing mandarin robes. The man in both these photos was a Hakka from the same region of China as my family. The same region, different circumstances.

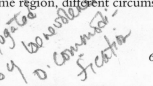

He migrated to Java in the 1850s in search of fortune. Providence that is often mistaken for a better life. Cheong Fatt Tze operated steamships between Medan and Penang and eventually became rich enough to be offered the post of vice-consul of China. At the height of his glory, he had eight wives. His trading empire was dotted with lavish residences, but this mansion was his principal home. It is built around an open space. In its courtyard, there is always a vegetal blossoming. A movement through porous layers and veils toward a communal desire. A movement toward a space of dreams. The birthplace of the carnal being. A being beyond the necessities of economy. In this city, the dreams of open spaces have become a privilege of mansions and villas. Buildings that can open their legs without fear of exposing a lack, a missing piece.

On Larut Road there is another mansion, this one immaculately maintained and gleaming white. Limburg Mansion. The father of the man who built it was born to a poor family named Lim and given up for adoption to a wealthier family named Phuah. Phuah Hin Leong worked as a boatman, ferrying goods and passengers across the North Channel that separated Penang from the mainland. One day, two European passengers left behind a bag of gold in his boat. Instead of taking the gold, Phuah waited for them on the same spot so he could return the bag to his *ang mo* customers —waited with either the fear of obedience or his own dream of the way the world would turn out. The Europeans were impressed with his honesty and gave Phuah a large tip, which he saved to build his own business. When he became wealthy enough, he was able to reclaim his original surname for his children. One of them hired the firm Wilson & Neubronner to design a monument to the family name in 1917.

The building they drew up, Limburg, still bears the name of its original owner, but not his image. Hanging over the second-floor veranda is a bright red banner painted with a portrait of Colonel Sanders. His serene gaze looks after us as we walk down the road, our bellies filled with silence.

    —How could you live on an island like this and not be susceptible to architecture? Well, maybe you become a bit used to it all eventually. But how can you leave here without knowing architecture's profound pleasures? Look at your brother.

    —Sometimes Luk says he thinks architecture is dead.

    —Wah. Rubbish.

    —Look at this building. It's dead.

    —No. It's still being used.

    —Yes, but it's stopped growing.

    —Its story is still being told.

Auntie is reticent to tell me stories at first, especially stories of origin. She is so unsure of facts, she says. The order of things becomes less and less clear to her as she gets older. But after a while, the stories trickle out.

    —What kind of building is that, Auntie?

    —Don't know *lah*. Devil house.

Auntie's words are stretched out by the warm drawl of the night, then stuffed back into the island's vernacular clip. She is speaking a language that originated in the same coastal port of China that my great-grandfather left. He and his older brother arrived here from Swatow, still adolescent, on their way to work the tin mines in Perak. Khoo Chee Leong and his older brother, Khoo Chee Wah, arrived in a Penang that was then part of the British Raj in India. The language they spoke became a merchant's language, traded across the region by restless migrants. It took on the patina of other places.

Different layers of historical time settled on it, not changing its structure but leaving behind an experience of diversity. The residue of a lived life. A dreamed life. A suffered life.

Imagine the port glistening for the two brothers as their boat slithered through the strait. A city that seemed, at first glance, to be in its infancy, with squat godowns and whitewashed storefronts. A city that seemed, at first glance, to promise them everything they demanded. A city that left them feeling as if they had eaten a good meal: salt and oil still on their tongues, fire in their bellies. The two brothers made it this far, nearly a month after they left Swatow, hungry, feverish, never daring to look up at the sky. Trying to forget what lay behind them. Dreaming instead of what lay beneath their floating bodies. Dreaming of what lay ahead.

The Khoo brothers, mutating codes carried across black waters by Ghee Hin coolie brokers. One of Penang's original secret societies, the Ghee Hin's influence spanned from southern China across the tip of the Malay peninsula. Their wealth accumulated through importing and controlling the unskilled labor that mined tin in Southeast Asia. The traces of their wealth are still on display in the site of their former headquarters, the Goh Hock Tong, Five Luck Villa. The trappings are almost tiring in their familiarity. Stenciled windowpanes. A rock fountain. Victorian cast-iron columns. Wood-carved panels. Grand staircase.

The potential for tin mining in the region was first recognized around 1850. Tin was mainly exported to China, where it was used to make silver-stamped joss paper. The Ghee Hin fought a war with a rival secret society, the Hai San, over the upcountry tin mines. The Khoo brothers arrived to see the war spill into the streets of Penang. From here they would be dispatched to Perak, but their departure was delayed for a few weeks. Long enough for a mob to beat Khoo Chee Wah to death at the entrance to the godown on Pengkalan Weld where the coolies he arrived with were housed. His funeral was the same day the Ghee Hin were defeated and the Hai San head, Chung Keng Kwee, was appointed Kapitan China, the head of the Chinese community, by the British Resident. When the British forbid secret societies in 1893, Hai San assets were channeled into architecture: the reconstruction of kongsi buildings and clan temples.

Chung Keng Kwee became known as the city's great connoiseur of architecture. Khoo Chee Leong became known as a survivor. Khoo took a wife in Perak who tired of the mines and convinced him to return to Penang to work the rubber planations. Chung took over the Ghee Hin headquarters at Five Luck Villa and installed his own ancestral temple there. A black iron statue bearing his likeness still stands behind the altar table. The layout of the temple itself is labyrinthine. Narrow corridors. Steep staircases almost too dangerous to use. But there is a certain pleasure in trying to walk through these perverse instruments of utility. The pleasure of violence. Behind the ancestral hall, in a secluded courtyard accessible only through a tiny eastern passageway, is an ancient well where first the Ghee Hin and then the Hai San disposed of their rivals.

—*You get pleasure out of knowing that?*

—Don't know *lah.*

—*I can imagine killing them. But it's the rest of it that's the problem. Their bodies. Disposing of them. The smell. The organs. All that liquid. Does that make sense to you?*

* * *

When we pass the State Museum on Farquhar Street, workers are still cleaning the statue of Captain Francis Light. Auntie says it was modeled on the features of his son. No picture of the man could be found. In 1786, Light, on behalf of the East India Company, acquired possession of Penang from the local sultan. He brought over thousands of Teochew, Hokkien, Hakka, and Tamil migrant workers, loaded his ship's cannons with silver dollars, and fired them into the jungle to encourage the men to hack back the undergrowth. The land was cleared for British fortifications and trade. Rivers muddied with gold collided with streams of blood and semen, eventually voiding into a great ocean of shit.

—*Why so quiet? You still thinking about that photo?*

—Probably.

It's not that I'm obsessed with finding this photo of my grandmother. It's just that I've never seen her. Did she even exist? Or is she just another one of the fragments of stories that my family passes around between silences? Stories prompted by my thirst for origins.

—*Your grandmother came to Penang to go to school. Her parents sent her to the Convent Garden School on Light Street, a girls' school that was founded by three French nuns.*

—*Your grandmother was a beautiful woman.*

—*Your grandmother was poor but by no means uncultured. By no means.*

—*Your grandmother was the only one of us who could read and write.*

—*Your grandmother loved your grandfather. He was working on the school grounds as a gardener.*

—*Your grandmother's mother came for the wedding, but not her father.*

But these are only crumbs, grudgingly fed to me. Cheap and unsatisfactory. Folks are so stingy with their memories of her. I can never understand why they would keep the full story from me. What they would hide from me.

It's just a story I want to hear. A story at the onset of the rainy season. A story like this. A gardener, sixteen years old, is crossing the green manicured lawns of the Convent Garden School. The air smells of watermelons. The gardener is carrying a shovel across his shoulders. Shoulders that seem to be drawn with the last traces of ink in the well. Overemphasized, they make the rest of his body look hungry in comparison. His hair is short, clean, crowned with a few beads of sweat. Two schoolgirls in matching uniforms are traveling on bicycles toward him down the same path. *There he is,* they whisper to each other at the same time. They giggle at the coincidence. The gardener tries to pretend he doesn't hear them, but their laughter has already inflected his rhythm. He leaves his body, watches it move, the pace now stiff and awkward. The girls sense his discomfort and are encouraged. As they get closer to him, they wave and smile. Their gestures are drawn with the same brush as the gardener's shoulders: strong and full of guile. The gardener hesitates. To wave back would be the wrong response. He doesn't want them to think he is undignified. To not wave back would be petty, the worst thing to be on this island. So the gardener looks them in the eye and nods his head, unsmiling. His hands do not move from the weight they are balancing on his shoulders. The girls look at each other and stop their bicycles, impressed and intrigued. The gardener waits a few seconds before he looks back and smiles. The girls both smile at the same time and giggle again at the coincidence before turning and riding away, muttering about the gardener's cheeky manners.

They are not manners accumulated through wealth or fortune or providence. The rich build themselves monuments to

[handwritten annotation: He looks for narrative in place that is the abolition of narrative]

mark their mortality. Windows into the timeless. The names of the victors are everywhere in the city. On street signs. Mansions. Markets. Ah Quee. Francis Light. Queen Victoria. The Earl of Carnarvon. Robert Townsend Farquhar. Sir Henry Gurney. Major General Archibald E. H. Anson. Cheong Fatt Tze. I look for the names of a Siamese schoolgirl and a gardener who is the son of a Teochew mine worker among the buildings of George Town. And, having failed that, I look for some reminder that the poor and the dead are not something that history merely goes through. I think I see the schoolgirl's face staring back at me from the fluorescent-lit remnants of the city. Try to make the buildings tell me a story. The story of who she was. I thought there were no more stories left to tell. But maybe there is still one.

120 Armenian Street, 67 Jalan Padang Kota Lama, 109 Lebuh Farquhar, 1865: The Khoo brothers, 1925: Le Arn Sayneevongse, 1820: Napoleonic war in Europe, 1820: British seize Dutch holdings in the Straits, 1874: Maharaja Lela assassinates British Resident Birch, 1895: Dato Bahaman tricked into surrender, 1937–1939: Persaudaraan Sahabat Pema (Brotherhood of Pen Friends), 1867: Tin wars in Perak, 1861: Surat Sungai (River Letters), 1823: Chu Tsai Thau (Heads of Piglets), 1823: Coolie Brokers, 1989: Fan blowing the hair on your belly, 1971: Your grandfather dies clutching your photograph, 1917: October Revolution, 1941: Malayan People's Anti-Japanese Army, 1945: Madame Khoo Siew Boei, 1949: Federation of Malaya, 1945: Communist Party of Malaya, 1950: The Emergency, 1952: Bedong Estate, 1952: Dublin Estate, 1948: Batang Kali, Selangor, 1950–1960: Briggs Plan, 1950–1960: British puncture tinned food, 1989: Everyone eats off of us.

Landscape. At the top of Penang Hill, above the Waterfall Temple, looking down through the haze at the deep greenery behind George Town, spreading out as far as you can see. On a small stone wall at the edge of the road, someone has spray-painted: *This view is dedicated to all those who died during the Emergency.* Clouds moving lazy across the sun. Rain across the strait. A storm in Medan.

Jockeying among the crowds near Pengkalan Weld, Auntie loses me. I wander through the tumult without her. Feel the warm skin of the moving crowd. Pushing. A boy with flawless shoulders and gleaming skin that disappears into greasy waves of black hair moves close. A pair of baggy jeans hangs off his hips, defying gravity, exposing the waistband of plaid boxer shorts. A square label, not LEVI'S but BLACK POWER, is stitched to the back pocket of his jeans. Invitations glisten on his cruel, lovely mouth. Without moving, his lips call for another time. Another place. Another world where interior and exterior flow together. Where structure dissolves into surface. Where comfort and abstractions inhale the same breath. His lips demand a total breakdown of law and order.

Maybe a building is not a body. Certainly not either of our bodies. Too volatile. A long time ago, perhaps on this same street as a child, I inhaled a grain of dust that is turning into a diamond in my throat. I feel it growing every day, still rough and unpolished, its sides slowly smooth against the heat of anger. Sometimes the fury that will make it beautiful threatens to incinerate the body that carries it. Even the memories of what inspired the fire are engulfed by it. Not to worry. There is no danger to innocent passersby. Not to worry. This body will not blossom into shrapnel. It will only implode in the touch of the fire.

Auntie is waiting for me where I should have known she would wait for me. At the bus stop.

—I was a little worried about you, she says, and then returns to the newspaper she was reading.

History of Breath

Ma, read to me. Again. The story. The story of how you saved me. How you took us out of the housing projects just before sunset. Left Ba to deal with the police himself. You knew you were dead if he ever found you again. No one calls the police on Ah Khoo. Try to explain again. How the gun he hid under your bed was intended for you. You tell the police this in your stuttering English. When they look puzzled, Luk and I raise our voices. We confirm everything fluently. Repeat the sounds that have lulled us to sleep for the last two years. Ba's voice smacking your face, his hands turning your flesh blue. The sound of the belt snapping. We tell the police it is all true. Your sorrow. Heaving. Water. Salt. Thin lyrics, whisper of smoke.

Ba and Ma leave behind an island that recedes into a hole. A piece missing from the continuous flow of history. They vanish. When his father dies, Uncle sends Ba a telegram, but there is rarely more communication between Ba and his family. Between Ma and hers. Between here and there. Home and exile. Ba could barely read anyway. Being away somehow made the domain of the written word draw tighter to exclude him. When I return, in his place, I'm asked to fill the emptiness with story. Sometimes the directness of the interrogation is surprising.

—Now tell me the truth. Did your parents get divorced?

What need for divorce? I want to tell them. *Ah Khoo makes his own laws.*

I tell them everything. Except I don't tell them he died almost two months ago.

you see

And if women

were equal

this kind of

You wouldn't have

poverty.

Ba works a number of jobs, each with less meaning than the one before. Then one day, without ceremony or sentiment, Ba falls off the economy. Uncle Tito cuts him in on a sideline, smuggling cigarettes and fireworks up from the Carolinas. After a few months, Uncle Tito warms to him. Introduces him to Uncle Ong. Ba gets a mechanic's job in one of Uncle Ong's garages in Queens. Chopping up stolen cars. Salvaging the parts.

He never beat Luk, but it's funny, because Luk is the one who didn't talk to Ba after he left. Neither did Ma, but you'd expect that. You were the only one. You tell no one he has died—

not Luk, not Ma, not Uncle. No one. It's your secret. Your final power over him. Cycle of birth. World without end. A pimp dies. Another is born. *who is the other one?*

The job falls on you to write his epitaph. Only you are there. He has no other family in Honolulu. No friends. His second wife went back to the mainland the day he died. Nothing left to keep her anymore. A few fellow night watchmen show up for the funeral. You hire a Catholic priest to perform the rites. You toyed with the idea of a Buddhist funeral, just to piss his ghost off, but a Catholic service is easier to arrange. He was adamant about being a Catholic. The service is quick. Faster than you thought it would be. But there is little to say here. Just throw a shovel of soil on his coffin. Keep a straight face. Thank the three men from his job site who showed up. None will see the epitaph you have had engraved on his tombstone when it is raised months later. Even you will not see it. You will be on a Thai Airways flight. In transit.

The only acknowledgment you make of tradition is to open his mouth and place his heavy gold ring in it. His tongue is dry and cold. Your hand lingers on his jaw as you push his mouth together. Watch his lips close like oil over light.

You don't know where the gun came from. Never saw it before. Maybe Uncle Tito gave it to him to hold. He never said. Ma still believes he was going to use it on her. Whatever. No one ever spoke about it after the arrest. Ma found it between the mattresses when she was cleaning. Or so she said. I saw the thing briefly. 357 Magnum. It might as well have been a land mine or one of the VRAM chips Martina produces in the Free Trade Zone. MADE IN USA. But that's the whole planet these days. The police put the gun in a plastic bag and took it out of the apartment before Ba came home. They took him the minute he came in the door. He smiled throughout the whole thing. Even when they snapped the handcuffs on him, he asked them politely to loosen them. Ma was in the other room with Luk. You were watching from the doorway. Remember Ba's face. His insistent smile like a mischievous beam. But as much as you tried to look at him, to get his attention, he wouldn't look at you.

Auntie takes me to Kek Lok Si to have my name written on a roof tile. She gives 10 ringgit to a woman behind a desk. A nun dabs out our Chinese names on a curved tile. The tile goes to cover the roof of a renovated part of the temple complex. Absorbed into the architecture.

Auntie leads me to the altar behind the nun. We kneel in front of the Goddess of Mercy. She bows.

I don't believe in religions.

She bows again.

Those who have power use them to oppress us.

She bows a third time.

I believe in God. But not in God's family.

Perhaps if we climb to the roof that shelters us, I can see my grandmother's name there. Perhaps there is some image of her in one of the vaults here that encloses the urns of the faithful. But Auntie reminds me that she was buried, not cremated. That the rains have probably long ago washed her name off the roof of the temple.

The faithful overflow into the streets around the mosque on Friday. Hundreds of backs. Shoulder to shoulder. Head to foot. On the sidewalk. The streets. Bridges. All bowing down as a single body. Traffic comes to a halt. The workday stops. Time fractured by a muezzin's call.

Chowrasta. The four crossroads. I stand in the temple court-yard at Green Lane with a cage. Inside the cage, two sparrows. Close my eyes. Move my lips. My throat. My neck humming with merit. *Pattidāna.* Raise the cage above my head. Face east. North. West. South. Lift the door. Open the way to every direction. Let the wind go through. The sparrows jump. Confused, they hop around for a bit, poking their heads at the space in front of them. The first dour smell of uncertainty. Its emptiness is itself a struggle. Against forgetting. A memory of space before desire. Before archi-tecture. Sky without buildings. Without limit. The fear caresses them. One bird leaps out of the cage, landing on the ground, jumping around frantically. The other flies into the wind.

The angel falls from a land without history. The angel falls on the city of the perpetual flight forward. A city with concrete already stained by dreams. Blood. Sweat. Semen. The angel with-out remembrance falls into the city to give history the monopoly of time. The angel comes to strip the imagination of its ability to undo time.

79

Consider East Asia in 1975. The United States was with-drawing from Vietnam, and many observers predicted that widespread instability would follow a broader American with-drawal from the region. Compare these predictions with the stable and prosperous East Asia of [today]. The important reasons that the gloomy predictions proved wrong were Ameri-can alliances in the region and the continued presence of sub-stantial United States forces. Security is like oxygen: you do not tend to notice it until you begin to lose it. The American security presence has helped provide this "oxygen" for East Asian development.

—United States Security Strategy
for the East-Asia Pacific Region,
Department of Defense, Office of International
Security Affairs, Washington, D.C.

The angel is made of matter. Fiberglass or flesh, it doesn't make a difference. Any matter will do. The angel carries a tablet given to him by God the Father. The tablet is engraved with the new laws of the millennium. The angel reads them out loud. The laws of matter. Laws with the quality of nature. Laws with no room for the spirit. The spirit has no value in this new world. Only matter has value, value that can be counted. The prohibitions and pleas of the spirit are ruled out by the priority of economic laws. The laws of pure speed. The angel takes his place on the lidded seat of a public toilet. You fall to your knees in front of him. Without smiling, he takes your arms and handcuffs them around the tank of the toilet. He rubs his cock across your mouth. Pushes it down your throat. Your hungry mouth covers it in spit. Cold. Dry. Needy. He comes. His wickedness lost in you as you silently utter

a wish. A wish to die a hundred times this way, the object of someone else's history.

Vitruvius said that the form of the temple should be analo-
gous to the character of the divinity. When you were younger,
Ma would insist that Ba take all of you to Kek Lok Si. Then, the
walkway to the temple was wide enough to accommodate the
faithful and a crew of beggars who sat in the shade of the temple
walls, empty plastic bowls lazy at their feet. The temple was always about stability. Its foundations rested on divinity. But its
architecture was always challenged by the restless, pained bodies
that flowed through it. Its structure was constantly challenged by
the processes of contemplation that it witnessed. Space activated
by movement. Hand dipped in pocket. Turned over coins and
lint. Triceps tightened. Hand tensed to drop a few coins into the
cup of a man in a T-shirt that said I'M A PROFESSIONAL BETA-TESTER
FOR MICROSOFT. Ba grabbed your hand angrily before you could
take it out of your pocket. *Don't give them money!* Ba warned sternly
as you looked around the temple. Every wall is a poem. A poem
about emptiness and the freedom from things. But in this garden
of liberation, Ma would always want to make an offering. Pass
some pennies on for joss sticks. Ba would always be angry when
she spent her money like this. His rage warmed you, comforted
you. Ba was always angry at Ma. Angry that she would transmit
these gestures to his children. It was the Sacred Heart of Jesus,
Limited, not the Kek Lok Si temple, that owned his home. Why
give money to an institution that did not house you? Ba would
stand outside the temple grounds, waiting for Ma. Outside, with
the beggars, while she expressed her own humility. *Why do you*

do that with your body? You don't need to do that. Ba could never understand the comfort of falling on bended knees.

Auntie buys a thin sliver of gold leaf. I watch it shine, wrinkle under my breath. She points me in the direction of the outdoor altar to Nang Kwak, her arm beckoning fortune, suitors, whatever. Her mother unknown. I move behind her. Raise both arms to the back of her foot. The front of the deity is covered with gold leaf so that her features are no longer discernible underneath. The edges of a few leaves curl up. In the breeze, they make a noise like the quiet burning of whole forests. Auntie clicks her tongue but says nothing. What a waste. No one will see it there. A new understanding of waste. What cannot be consumed. What cannot contribute to consumption. In the courtyards of the temple, belief becomes merit. Another system of accrual.

Love Lane. No one quite knows why it's called this. A little street once inhabited by Eurasians who used the nearby church at Farquhar Street. Possibly, it was where sailors met local prostitutes. Or where rich men kept their mistresses. Or it may have been about a different kind of love. Love among the convicts and soldiers the British brought from north India. During the Muharram festival, these Shia Muslims commemorated the death of Ali, the son-in-law of the prophet, and his sons Hassan and Hussain. Devotees would flagellate themselves with chains and whips. Pierce their flesh with hooks, swords, skewers. Walk on coals. The procession went down Chulia Street and up Love Lane before heading toward the north beach for ritual ablutions. It was in Love Lane that their voices lifted to recite the names of the martyrs. Flow of bodies and blood. Familiar migrations. This time for a different reason. For the love of Hussain.

Late in the night, even though I can no longer see her, I can still hear Ma working. I can hear her moving through what I think are my dreams. The flicker of light from her room illuminates the faces of long-buried beauty. Stone faces that guard the walls of temples, now crisscrossed with vines and mortar. The sound of her labor into the night becomes my solace. My lullaby. My pillow of noise.

Ma stopped praying after she left Ba. *Nothing left to pray for,* she said. Nothing left to ask for. It's easier to describe our world in prayers than to help ourselves. But even our descriptions are flawed. Moving around in the world, it's still not visible to us. To really see the world is to be free of it. But the world is made from me. I begin from that arrogance. I am not made from the world.

I still believe Ma loved Ba. On the altars of longing. In the garden of liberation. In my dreams, she lights the sticks, three of them. Brings the flame above her forehead, down to her heart in one arc. The flames descend into embers. She kneels in front of the altar, her legs tucked around to the side, her head inclined. She brings her head down to the floor. The icon sitting on the table in front of her is a patinaed bronze or decayed gold. It is old and has not been replaced since my grandmother brought it here before the war. Ma's skin is fair and, standing next to Ba, gleaming sandalwood, she bore the radiance of an ear of corn. In my dreams she has her own fantasies. *I dream about your father sometimes,* she tells me. *Sometimes the dreams are good. Sometimes they're bad*. She tells me she is unlike Ba because she never became a Catholic. In this part of the world, Jesus is made of white plaster. She could never see the sense of kneeling in front of a statue that was lighter than her husband.

The tombstone. I never saw it. I can imagine it. His name: Khoo Eng Theng. His life: 1936–1989. His epitaph: AND YOU CAN GO ON.

Comes Love
Nothing Can Be Done

It has been more than a few days since I last saw Thong. Tonight, his skin is rolling around in my throat. With the raw smell of rotting vegetation and burned-out oil pouring in from the back window. Crumpled around a pillow in sweat, my eyes cut through closed lids to the ceiling above my head. How many times had I seen this ceiling as a child and wondered if this was the sky that could contain me. Sky falling on shoulders. Enormity pressing down. The rest of the family is asleep, but sleep for me is impossible tonight. I turn on the light. It has been nearly a week since I last saw Thong, and each time the light goes on I am surprised to find that the bed is not soaked in my own blood. I am trying to remember what he feels like, so I can fall asleep with that filament of a dream. It would never be enough to merely describe his skin. I would always mistake that description— superficial, gloating of conquest—for the actual experience of touching him. If I said his skin was soft, that banal softness would forever eclipse the tactile grace of running my hand across his flesh. Flesh that felt more like liquid. Skin that deceived my fingers into thinking they were dragging through some volatile cloud of mercury. Skin that yielded, inviting my fingers to push, probe against something that dared them to slip through its pores, and then resisted, pushing back. Skin that made me promise loyalty. Commitment. Faith. Skin that made me lie. Leaving him only smudged underneath my fingernails. Dissolving on my tongue. Caught between my teeth. Every night without him I learn new lessons. I learn that love is not a feeling but a language made entirely of actions.

The departure is never as orderly as it's been planned. The helicopters never take off in a straight line from the roof of the American embassy. They tilt with the weight of desperation, that cloying desire to remain in the thick, hairy arms of security. But every refugee is only dispatched into further uncertainty. Every refugee flies deeper into a half-true sky of unkeepable promises. Cast adrift at Site 9, knowing there's no return but no future either.

Don't ask me why I'm trying to write him a postcard. Him of all people. He set the cycle moving. If Jim hadn't expelled me, I would never have felt the responsibility of tending to my father's demise. I would never have had the strength to come back here. His home, its spare calm, its expensive dignity, was too comfortable to ever think of leaving. The last time I saw him was at the Tombs, when they released me. I never returned any of the messages he left for me after that. Messages that ended with *I want you back* or *No one will ever love you the way I love you*. Part of Jim's power over me was language. He owned the words he used. He could use them without imagination. Without the pretense of beauty.

I thought I could write him a letter from here. Answer him once and for all. Instead, I find myself starting the same letter again and again. It's a letter I sometimes finish but never mail. It's a letter that is reborn every day.

86

One afternoon, I take a series of buses to a part of town I have never been in before. The walls are covered with government murals championing the new antidrug initiatives, aimed mostly at small-time addicts and pushers. They echo something Luk had told me about his flight into Penang last year. Upon landing, the stewardess cheerfully announced the local time, temperature, and penalties for drug smuggling. "*Dadah* is death. Have a nice day." Across from one mural is a coffee shop, empty of customers. A thin coating of grease hovers over the tabletops: pale mottled-blue Formica. An old man with a large parchment-skinned face shuffles over when I sit down and passes over a cup of milky sweet Nescafé.

—*It's all that's left, son.*

In every fantasy that Jim would spin about me, he would always begin by describing our surroundings. "I imagine you in a house with a balcony. . . ." I begin my postcard to him with a description of my surroundings: *A sleepy city on a tropical island.*

Stop. Too banal. A dingy coffee shop in a forgotten part of George Town, as the sun goes down. Yesterday was Christmas. It is hard to believe the day has passed without event. But in this part of the world, the days leading up to it are more important. The birth of the Christ child is less important than the gifts the black kings brought him. The straw of his manger will always be eclipsed by the tinsel still up on the walls, next to the ANNIHILATE JUNKIES signs. It's only a few days before the new year. Time for a new beginning. A clean break.

Perhaps that is how the situation will resolve itself even without my interference. Without my postcard. Jim refused to let me back into the apartment anyway. He said the clothes and books I had left there were rightfully his. He had paid for them.

Narrator had abandoned companion (handwritten annotation)

If I wasn't going to live among them anymore, I had no right to them. But Jim made it clear the door was still open for my return. Anytime I was ready to come to my senses and reinhabit his valuable crib, I could again wear the vestments of my position as his worthy companion. Jim had taken many pictures of me in those clothes, amid his other prize possessions: Giacometti coffee tables, Biedermeyer chairs. They were pictures he was proud to show me once they had been developed. *Part of my appreciation of your beauty is photographing you,* he told me. *I want to show you how beautiful you are.*

Jim and I had not exchanged words, much less photographs, since the night I was arrested. There were only hysterical and enraged recordings left in places we thought the other might retrieve them. Luk ran into him occasionally. He was usually in the company of some unknown youth, darker, younger, more wide-eyed than the last one. Predictable, really. Too predictable. His latest diversion was with him now in Paris.

I leave a few coins on the table by my empty coffee cup and thank the owner as I leave. He raises his hand without speaking, inhaling a deep curl of smoke. I wonder if this new plaything of Jim's is being treated as well as I was in Paris. It was on that trip that Jim first used my body as a mirror, sucking back lines of coke off every surface that would support them and licking up the residue in those crevices where they fell. Jim always said that cocaine made him feel as if he were unencumbered by his body. It left him free to indulge in mine. My own body is starting to return to itself in these weeks since I left him. I can feel the blood starting to circulate more willfully, gleefully, in my veins. I have been in Penang for almost a week, surrounded by family but essentially living alone with my body. I think I can do things with it now that I never knew I could do. The slightest changes in light and temperature register on my skin, make the pores dilate or snap shut. I start having what I think are olfactory hallucinations. I can smell something burning from miles away. Sometimes I confuse the various sites of my body and their functions. The hairs on my legs can smell the salt in the air. Every time my heart beats, I swear I can see it, torn beating from my chest and still throbbing inside a butcher's refrigerated display case. Every time I breathe, a train derails. Hardly any part of my body has escaped damage from miracles these past few days.

And then I remember Jim is returning from Paris on the eighteenth.

I walk over to a pay phone by the post office. Find the number for the American consulate in a directory.

—I'd like to report a drug smuggler.

The Malay operator wordlessly transfers me to an older, businesslike male voice.

—He's about six foot one. Blond. American passport. His name is James Conrad. He's arriving in New York from Paris on the eighteenth. Probably Air France.

—Do you want to give your name?

—No. Of course not.

I hang up.

The postcard is completed before my turn at the post office. Two words on an empty square of cardboard.

Keep everything.

I buy my stamps. *Mel udara ke Amerika Syarikat.* There's a mailbox outside the post office that swallows my postcard with as little effort as I wrote it. A pebble lodges itself between my foot and slipper, and as I bend to dislodge it I wonder at how dirty my feet have become. This ground. More than landscape. More than a scenic backdrop for my own travels. This ground has left its indelible stain on my skin.

I walk to the bus stop. Wait for the long journey back to Tanjong Tokong to begin. It feels as though everyone is staring at me. My face. They can read something terrible on it. Pigeons soar through the disappearing sky. The streets are decidedly empty after Christmas and at twilight; the birds only underscore the return to the island's easy pace of solitude. Two Malay schoolgirls stand silently apart from the line waiting for the bus. White scarves are pristinely fastened around their cherubic faces, the edges touching the back of their blue skirts. Perched at the curb, they stand with their feet balancing dangerously over the street. Half on the sidewalk, half in space. As if they too could fly away.

Kurang Manis:
Less Than Sweet

It is raining when I meet my cousin at the factory gates, across the road from the kampung mosque. The rain is barely noticeable, a light windless tattoo on my skin, but Martina still carries her umbrella like a shield as she leaves the factory court-yard. I have seen her once, years before, a smart-mouthed school-girl who made fun of the way I spoke. Now she is working the assembly lines of the Free Trade Zone. She has lost the clarity of her age, but not the look. Her face is still cruel. Sinewy and alive. Not easy to pick out from among the other young women who leave the components factory with her at the end of the workday.

They work in overlapping seven-hour shifts through the night, into the time of dreams. Leaving the factory, their gossip is cheerful, almost relieved, but Martina insists it belies more somber recent events. I overhear them easily as they walk past me. The factory is possessed, she says confidently, almost proudly. In the last two weeks, fourteen women have been escorted from the shop floor after going into shock and convulsions during their shifts. During the latter half of the nineteenth century, when the industrial workday was introduced to this part of the world, the British Resident in Malaya, Hugh Clifford, described a psycho-pathological disorder common among the Malay subjects of the colony called *latah*. Any sudden noise, shock, or command could bring on the affliction, in which subjects were unable to realize their own identity. Often, the person suffering from *latah* could only imitate the actions of others, accompanied by cursing and swearing. It's been said that anyone bold enough to attract the attention of someone suffering from *latah* can make them do anything by simply feigning it. Although not familiar with the psychological discourse of his day, Clifford believed this seed of disorder grew in every native.

—You hungry? Martina chides. Of course you are.

We walk down to the Ring Road, where several stands line the perimeter of a coffee shop. Only one is still open. Martina makes me sit down at a dented tin table and goes over to the stand. A wide, rubbery man in scratchy black shorts and plastic slippers asks me what we're drinking. I order a Carlsberg for myself, and Martina calls out for an *air bali*. He brings it back just as Martina settles onto her stool. Her hair is cut just below her ear, a shiny pageboy she keeps wrapped under a scarf at work.

—*These women.*

She doesn't lower her exasperated voice. No need to. Most of the women she works with cannot speak Teochew.

—*It is not nice the way they try to copy men.*

I noticed a few of them, their hair cut even shorter and more boyish than hers, sauntering confidently out of the factory at the end of the day.

—*Like, they want to be rugged. They see men wearing baggy jeans and basketball jerseys. They want to do the same. They forget their sex.*

Another man arrives at the table with two bowls of Hokkien *mee*. I tear into mine. Martina laughs.

—*Boys only know how to eat.*

—So, Martina, I manage between mouthfuls.—So, Martina, how do you forget you are a woman?

—You forget your femininity.

—And what's that?

—Femininity is everything that isn't masculine.

She might as well say, *A game that is described by its gestures.* The better part of our lives are days filled with them: small, intimate, and confining. The significance of those gestures is gleaned later, after the fact of our labors. It's only the rituals that have lost their meaning: Auntie making *puja* at the start of the day, planting three burning joss sticks upright in a tin cup in front of the house. Auntie boiling the drinking water in the morning, doing the laundry, cooking. Rituals I cannot participate in, except to consume their benefits: a cup of coffee, a plate of lunch, clean clothes. I used to watch Martina do these things also, helping her mother with the daily routines of sustaining a household. But these days her hands attend to less domestic rituals. Martina's days are spent moving Palette DAC and VRAM chips on their journey down an assembly line. The movement of fingers and wrist only superficially resembles that of Auntie in the kitchen. When Martina started working in the factory, she says she was both awed and intrigued by the equipment she had to use. The microscope she needed to see what her hands were doing was an instrument she had only seen scientists and professors use on television.

—*Now I just look at the microscope and want to smash it.*

This past month, her bosses have endeavored to raise production quotas in the factory.

—*We work three shifts sometimes. By the time the midnight shift comes, we are tired. Still, we have to use that microscope. It feels like we've been tricked, you know. Sometimes we scratch words on the microchips.*

She smiles. A thin ray across her face that makes an accomplice out of anyone who can see it.

—*Bad words.*

Martina's right eye presses against the rim of the microscope, dilating against the light coming through the other end. A city coalesces. Cities of digital imperfection cross the forest of dark fingers. Cities built on the swell of night. Out of the fantastic mucus of the brain. Dotted with temples beyond art. Beyond splendor.

A glimpse of madness. The defiance of reason. When European adventurers stumbled on the ruins of Angkor Wat in the middle of the Khmer jungles, they were terrified. They ferried back descriptions to the metropole that sounded like the labyrinths of hell. I see it in photographs they have made of the temple at the turn of the century. The beginnings of reclaiming the thousand faces of the Bayon from the jungle. What is beautiful about Angkor Wat in these images is the way the banyan trees have entwined themselves among the ruins, keeping them together in a state of slow and fluid decay. A dynamic entity, pulled from the anarchy of dreaming sleep. But it is also possible to see in that chaos the ruins of a more pastoral utopia. A city shielded from contagion.

As in any city, the random access memory that flows down the assembly lines of the Free Trade Zone takes its cues from the souls that feed it, lapsing from their endless journey only long enough to wither into bone. Krakatoa lost in a river of lava. Angkor Wat in the inevitability of the jungle. Babylon, city of sin destroyed by God or a mystified market collapse. We revel in the ashes of those empires until we succumb to the childish need for human warmth. The false and fleeting feeling of stability. Then we rebuild our settlements of lust. The city beckons, a pair of lips that sucks the life out of you. A mouth that vomits despair and desire across ruined circuits of beach and forest.

In the networks at Martina's fingertips, everything can now be regulated. Observed and controlled in a way that life in the

forest never was. Before this island became a backwater or a Free
Trade Zone, it was one of the most cosmopolitan cities in Asia.
Before Angkor became ruins, it was the heart of empire. Cities
built on trade routes always settle into dust. They get buried under
lava flows or strangled by banyan trees. Cities built on trade settle
into memory when the trade takes another direction. Now that
commerce is moving off the recognized paths and vanishing into
space, the cities are following them.

—*It's not a bad life, you know. I am earning my keep now. I feel
like an adult. But that factory. Something is not right.*

The rain has quickened its tempo, drumming its fingers
across the tin roof of the *kedai kopi*. Our bowls are empty but I
stab occasionally into the red broth shaking in the bottom of mine.

—*The women say they saw* hantu.

—What kind of *hantu?*

She doesn't answer. Pretends she doesn't understand me.
When I ask again, she says she doesn't know.

A spirit moves easily through walls, across borders. A spirit
is a traveler moving between human and nonhuman domains.
There is never a single kind of spirit. *Toyol* are sprites who help
their masters reap wealth out of the air they breathe. *Pontianak*
birth demons threaten the life of newly born infants. Then there
are possessing spirits. The spirits of the original inhabitants of the
land, the people grouped in tribes and animals, roam old burial
grounds, strangely shaped rocks, hills, and trees. Spirits deemed
evil by Islam are everywhere. If a woman lacks in spiritual vigi-
lance and wanders into the sacred homes of spirits, she becomes
possessed. These spirits live in places that mark the boundary
between human and natural worlds. Two worlds, goes the story
passed on from resident to native. Two worlds, and there is always war at the border.

But the border is an apparition too, a strategic fiction to break the world down into concepts, spaces, limitations. I look back up the road to the factory and the mosque across from it. The factory is a body made entirely of dense, hard muscle, a solid chunk of meat with no suggestion of interior life. The mosque challenges me to look. I have always had a hard time looking at mosques. They were the monuments to Malaysia's official culture, a culture that would always leave me outside. During prayer times, I would avert my eyes, a nonbeliever, but still strain to listen to the muezzin's call, its lyric marking the movement of time. Today I look—not at the arches or the minaret or the tin dome, but the graceful cavities they claim as relations. Time and space are a part of the building as surely as they are a part of us. But the factory owners know the most productive time is a territory, a schedule, a mere dimension to portion and track. Martina's time is now a splinter in the machinery of the nation.

Martina shows me a photograph she keeps in her wallet. It's the two of us, actually. In it, I am her older cousin, standing awkward under a palm tree with her on the beach. If not for the photograph, I would never remember this moment. A memory made retrievable and at our disposal.

Hantu are the memories that cannot yet be bought. That cannot be stilled in the glossy surfaces of a photograph or a DAC chip. The ghost of our common grandmother wanders unfettered by a photograph. She is seen occasionally along the assembly lines of the Free Trade Zone, stooped and gray as she never lived to be, barefoot and puffing on a cheroot. She leans over the faces of the neophyte workers, touching their skin with her ashen fingers. She can glean the inner workings of a person this way. She can tell who has fled her kampung, pregnant and unmarried. Who dares not return home because of her father's repeated sexual advances. Who

96

is scraped and emptied. She knows well these women who are learning what it means to be treated like a thing. Who in some ways
have never known anything else. She knows them and smiles, the
cheroot bouncing at the corner of her mouth. An ash descending.
Ghost dancing in the machine. Thorn lazy on the narrow path of
progress. Collective bargaining as spirit possession.

Hear her tell it:

> *August 10, 1990—A Penang-based American microelectronics*
> *factory had to be shut down for the third day in a row today due*
> *to women claiming they were possessed by spirits. Some girls*
> *started sobbing and screaming hysterically, and when it seemed*
> *like it was spreading the other workers in the production line*
> *were immediately ushered out. It is a common belief among*
> *workers that the factory is* kotor *and supposed to be haunted by*
> *a* datuk. *One morning one of the operators was found uncon-*
> *scious in the women's bathroom. When she came to, she told of*
> *how she had seen a demon with a three-foot tongue licking sani-*
> *tary napkins in the bathroom.*

Women start imagining the unimaginable: What would it
be like to be a human being? Only by making the native inhuman
did the British Resident become human. Only by participating
in the inhumanity of the workday will the native earn her humanity. Labor allows her to know herself, to know subjugation
and alienation. Without labor, the native is just an unprofitable
element in the fabric of the empire, incapable of developing the
colonies' resources. The native becomes neither human nor machine, but both. A winged cypher with a smoking shotgun. She
lives on the outskirts of salvation, far south from the neon crosses
of heaven and the Sacred Heart of Jesus, Limited.

[handwritten: commodity valorization → human]

—You know, I don't love this job, but that paycheck makes me feel more human.

She sighs.

—But what is human these days, anyway?

We rise when we see the bus coming down the road, the bus that will take us home. We wait for a while under the awning of the *kedai kopi* as the rain continues its merciless rhythm. Then we run across the road, the rain falling across our face like firecrackers. We board the minibus, savoring the sting of the air conditioner. A wet shirt stirring across my chest. The rain fleeing my hair. Every drop of water that tumbles down reflects the secret of the world's weird and terrifying beauty. The angry tilt of a schoolgirl's hips, the pockmarked flesh of the minibus driver, even my own cousin's face: they all fall into focus in alarmingly sensuous detail. We rarely, if ever, comment on the weather, but this afternoon Martina dares as we climb into our seats.

—You learn to take comfort in the rain.

The sound of traffic moving on wet streets.

Papo Mafia

[handwritten: him who?]

Please wipe the blood off the corner of my mouth. It's
unladylike. People will think I devour my prey whole. Nothing
could be further from the truth. I asked him to cut only a little
piece of himself off every day. Wash it in the sink, seal it in an
envelope, and send it south, across the border. It will be the only
proof I have of his existence. The only proof beyond his name.
The one piece of him I can carry. Remind him to keep the piece
little. Small and discreet. There are penalties for indiscretion down
south. In the morning papers, the names of Muslim youth caught
in indecent proximity to one another are exposed. *Khalwat.* A
beautiful name for sin. A word that is just a desire. An invitation
for shame, cut in Arabic into the fronds of a banana tree. Or a
punishment engraved in stone in the master's language. A fine. A
stroke or two of the rattan. Public stoning. Depending on the
severity of the crime. Under the sun, it is a crime to love without
reproducing the plantation's labor force.

Purpose governs every muscle here. At the border of the
known world, every movement is interrogated, every migrant
asked to produce proof of purpose. *Proof of purchase.* My days, lately,
are without either. On Wednesday I ask Ah Guan to take me to
Pulau Tikus for no good reason. He is one of my only cousins
who still makes his living like his father did, fishing. The boats

[handwritten right margin: that you are commodity]

[handwritten bottom: sex for pleasure sake = criminalized]

seldom stop at Pulau Tikus, a small stretch of sand and stone off the north coast of Penang. I went there as a child, over a decade ago. Even then, it was a favorite spot for illicit trysts.

I meet Ah Guan at the Tua Pek Kong temple in Tanjong Tokong. He is unsmiling and somber as he leads me a few steps away to his boat. He makes me sit in the back with the nets, near him, as he maneuvers the boat out into the strait. The thin boat skims across the water, gusts of salt water lapping at my skin. The day is sitting on the flat sea in shrouds of wet heat. We can barely see the coast of Butterworth. We have been out in the boat for ten minutes before we see the rocks of Pulau Tikus in the distance. He cuts his motor as we enter the cove on the east side of the island. The boat glides quietly onto the white beach, littered with garbage. I jump off the side of the boat, to show him that I can do those kinds of things, that my days may be without purpose but I can still work. I make a loud splash by the bow of the boat and push it back out. Ah Guan laughs, finally, at my clumsiness. Then he turns out of the cove, leaving me here for a few hours while he drops his nets in the sea.

At the apex of Pulau Tikus there is still a small *kramat,* a shrine housing a bed that is covered with lavish bolts of *songket.* One in particular catches my eye. A field of green and purple bruises, a plaid shot through with rivers of gold. A familiar excitement passes over my body. It is the same elation I feel whenever I pass a beautiful boy lying by himself on the beach, waiting for something to happen, and think, *How easy, anyone could steal this.* The thin rays of sun that shoot from the shuttered windows reveal the *songket*'s flawless weave, tight and impenetrable like a flag. In hand, in another light, another place, it might lose that quality. It might become a part of daily life, to be as taken for granted as our routines. In the end I pass on, move back from the bed, my hands only curling around sweat before I press them together and raise them to eye level.

When he first took me to this Muslim shrine, my uncle Ah Seng showed me how to do this. Pranom: an act of respect. Anyone can ask for intercession here, even if they are not Muslim. Everyone can pay homage to this bed. But it's not the power of the all-seeing, absolute and transparent, that keeps my hands pressed together instead of grabbing at *songket*.

Look at the bed again. Notice the dust and ashes. It's hard to say who is being respected here. A pirate, perhaps. A popular sultan disgraced by the British or the martyred wife of a cruel rajah. No one could say for sure. Fishermen like Ah Seng had been bowing their heads here for generations. The steps leading to the shrine, though, are covered with graffiti. *I LIKE TO EAT PUSSY. RAPE ME. NIRVANA. IN UTERO. BE HERE AT 11 PM SATURDAY TO SUCK MY BIG BLACK DICK. AHMED.* The scrawls form a map to islands in a constellation that span the world.

Pulau Tikus was once part of a global network that connected desire and belief. Islam, Hinduism, and Buddhism came through these networks, along with merchandise. When European ships arrived here in the sixteenth century, it wasn't a rustic clearing of disorganized natives they found but a highly developed mercantile class. A community that imported and exported commodities on an independent basis, supplying its own capital, financing transactions, organizing shipping on a global scale, and using the most advanced vessels of the time to reach distant places. Over the next turns of history, exploiting the rifts of difference and discontent, Europeans enforced a strict monopoly on goods at the ports, where their influence was all-powerful. They forced the region's produce to flow through their hands exclusively. In this way, a handful of small European powers destroyed the trading classes and consolidated their rule in the name of corporations. The Dutch East India Company, McDonald's, Shell, Motorola. The economy of the region became dependent on their distant but familiar capitals: London, Madrid, Rotterdam, Paris, New York, Tokyo. The ports became deserted, the revenues destroyed, the people reduced to slavery, the authority of the local sultans weakened by the arrogance and tyranny of the European visitor. The Europeans, after destroying the trading classes, accused the natives of having no interest in commerce and exchange. The natives were indolent and lazy, born criminals. The only recourse for the native was to follow the European example. The sultans grabbed back what they could. But the Europeans, having sucked all available trade into their own settlements—Penang, Singapore, Batavia—became obnoxious about the attacks of those they had driven to such courses. They gave the name of piracy to actions they themselves undertook without shame. The sultans did little to control the piracy, knowing that once a king allows poverty to arise in his nation, the people always steal to survive.

I close the door to the shrine behind me. Walk down steps clotted with sand. Look out over the littered beach for Ah Guan's boat. Lie under a palm tree in the cold sand. Close my eyes in spite of myself.

Ba was the first thief you knew. By his own admission, you were his best accomplice. He taught you there was no law to respect other than a law of averages. You would drive to the places he worked at night. Enter and unload things from the warehouse. When Ma asked where they came from, he would just say, *They fell off the truck.* You had seen things fall from moving vehicles. You couldn't imagine television sets, stereos, school clothes, games, and

kitchen appliances falling off a truck intact, but Ma had no problem believing it. In a new country, you make your own belief.
These objects gave you dignity in a place that was constantly trying to rob you of it, constantly trying to make your neck bend
under some imaginary pressure, trying to keep your face from
feeling the sun. Crime gave you dignity, made you feel human.
That is to say, it made you feel alive. You thought for a long time
about what it meant to fall off a truck. To be left behind in the
wake of its engine, roaring down the highway. You wondered if
your family hadn't fallen off a truck. It had seemed for a while
like Ba was driving the vehicle, hurtling through space, across three
worlds, quite a distance, but your life after a few months had taken
on the quality of being left behind. There was a great distance
now between what your family had expected and what you were
living. Between the images you were proffered continuously and
your own bodies. Your bodies were actually disappearing, like
the cities you lived in. They were being replaced by ghosts, objects, rubble. For every desire in the city, a building fell, so that
soon you were all living in a place of new ruins, picking among
them for the last vestiges of yourselves that had fallen off the truck.

Waves lick the soles of my feet. High tide. It is still Wednesday. Still long enough to feel the day unwinding under the sun,
the sweat drying in my pores.

The pirates of the region were known as "fishers of men."
In the anthroethnographic photography of the period, the men
are stripped and stilled. They stand slightly bewildered and naked
for the camera. It is possible to study the scale of their bodies

precisely, as one would study any building or object, down to the fractals. Down to the bone. The English photographer John Lampray placed the bodies of native men across a grid. The clear white chalk stretching tight and perfect across black orders the body just as it orders the city. Orders and defines. When the grid is emptied, it becomes a net.

In Malacca, on the eve of the English invasion of Java, Sir Thomas Stamford Raffles presented two boxes of opium to his emissaries, Tengku Penglima Besar and Pengeran. Europeans like Raffles didn't smoke opium themselves but traded in it and spread its use. Europeans like Raffles forbade it in their own countries. But in the colonies addictions were encouraged, especially among the unskilled workers who were shipped in from China, India, and Indonesia. The first British merchants in the Peninsula were opium dealers. Gambling, opium smoking, and toddy drinking made up a considerable part of the colonies' revenues. In some years, more than half of the revenue of the Malayan colony came from the sale of opium. The British Empire at the beginning of the nineteenth century was basically a drug cartel. Penang and Singapore were its stellar opium ports. Everything in the colony was built on its smoke, whole nations raised on its foundations. But smoke is only the sign of the smoker. Coolie. You've heard the term before. So many times that its meaning has been erased. *Ku li*. Hardship labor. Frame built on smoke. Salted fish. Rice. The residue still lingers in your tissues. A trace of something that bubbles up on your tongue at inopportune moments. No matter what clothes or perfume you wear to mask it, someone will always pick it out. Luk's colleagues search your face suspiciously when it surfaces. The bounce of a vowel. The clumsy breath between sentences. The hesitation before answering and then the speed with which the answer is doled out. The dialect that rings with an addiction to things and impatience at the industrial work ethic that is supposed to deliver them. *Your grandfather worked himself to death, and for what?* Ba would hiss when he saw you hesitate at taking something for nothing.

You would like to believe that was the sentiment in Le Arn Sayneevongse's family when your grandfather announced his intention of marrying her. *He is getting something for nothing.* Ah Mah's father would know. A Phuket merchant, he wanted her manicured for a better life. He insisted she attend a European school in Penang to improve her lot. What a mess that turned out to be. A gardener for a husband. Life in a tin-roofed shack on land leased from the Sacred Heart of Jesus, Limited. Ah Mah's father refused to attend the wedding. He sent his wife with the dowry stitched into her jacket. *Something for nothing.*

That is how you felt when you were with any number of men. *I am getting something for nothing.* Even if you tried not to show it, you were grateful. There was no real dowry involved, but the exchange was always tipped in your favor. It didn't matter what they looked like or how boring their affections became. Just their desire was enough. You could live under that roof. Easy. You could live in that kind of friendship. Friendships like a GI's candy bar. Sweet and lethal opportunities. *Friendship* was the name of a trading ship from Salem, seized by the villagers of Kuala Batu on the west coast of Sumatra in 1831 after some Yankee cheating. The next year, the president of the United States sent the frigate *Potomac* there to destroy the village in reprisal for violating the terms of the friendship.

It never occurred to you before what friendship would be like with someone who was like you. Outside the law. Now you struggle to name it. You and Thong will always face each other without terms or convenient words. You face each other with nothing to assure you about the meaning of the movement that carries you across oceans and borders. That carries you toward each other. He and you have to invent a relationship that is still formless. Have to invent a friendship outside laws, rules, and habits. A friendship that is like a building, but neither the skyscrapers going up nor the shop houses coming down. A building that was not meant to blissfully house the domestic from the public. Its materials are something else. Its bricks are your tongue in his ear, his chin brushing against your chest, your breath in his hair. This building is made of everything through which you can give each other pleasure. It is still under construction. It will take a long time to build. They do not issue permits for this kind of building. There is no model or blueprint for its construction. There is not even a name. This kind of crime is not included in the term *khalwat*. This kind of building is not described by the word *home*. But an idea that is not formulated in a name can still exist. It finds expression in other forms.

The splutter of Ah Guan's motor in the distance. Getting closer. Returning.

Stain

I found you. On the road to the beach at Batu Ferringhi. The man selling you had no interest in me as a customer. He was busy with some German tourists, trying to persuade them to buy a lamp. *Antique, antique,* he kept on saying. He didn't press you on me. I chanced upon you, flipping through a box of portraits. There you were. You could be any grandmother. There is a shape to your face, a certain difficulty in your smile, that reminds me of my own face in the mirror. I asked the man how much. He said 30 ringgits, and it made me smile. I put you down, but would never leave without you.

—Without the frame?

—*Twenty* ringgit.

—So the frame is only ten ringgit?

—Yes.

—Is that your best price? Can't you give me a discount, uncle?

I call Auntie over. She is a shrewd consumer. Never leaves the shop until the merchant is as exhausted as she. She whines mercilessly.

—*Come on, this is an old photograph. How can you think of charging twenty ringgit?*

—*It's a Nyonya,* the dealer insists. *Photographs of Nyonya are very hard to find. More expensive.*

Not just any Nyonya, I want to say, but I don't. Look at you. Your hair pulled back into a crown of pearls. A high collar sticks out from under the batik coat, fastened with three gold buttons. Your hands rest firmly on the knees of your *baju*. For a Nyonya, you are not wearing as much jewelry as you've been reputed. To make up for your personal lack, there is a money tree, fashioned out of gold, in a pot by your shoulder. Clouds gather in the mountains behind your head, but the landscape behind you is a lie, cheated inside a photographer's studio. There is a low wall painted on the backdrop behind you, to suggest you are sitting in your garden. The cornices of the wall are familiar. I see them on the fringes of George Town, propping up old mansions that have since been abandoned or converted into corporate offices. You sit at the edge of a wooden chair, your feet on a carpet. Underneath the carpet, there are some tiles, carved like lotuses. When I have exhausted you, taken in every detail of this photograph, I realize how small it is. Indeed.

—It's such a small photograph, even if it is a Nyonya. How about fifteen ringgit?

Auntie stops talking. I know she thinks even this price is expensive. After all, it's just a piece of paper. She doesn't even know this woman.

—You really want this photo?

She picks it up, trying to glean its value.

—Yes, but not the frame.

The man jumps at the opportunity.

—Fifteen ringgit.

He repeats the sum and sets to freeing you from your frame. He puts you in a plastic bag, tapes you shut, and hands you to me. Entrusts you to me. Auntie looks at you again, through the cloudy plastic bag. The man now shows me other pictures. Photos of other

Nyonyas. Of a group of immaculately dressed Chinese men in Paris. It's actually a postcard, the back inscribed with a description of the setting: *In the Université de Lyon, 1937, Kim Cheang Cheah and classmates from Penang.* That's when I flip you over and see what is printed on the back: POST CARD   CARTE POSTALE   CARTOLINA POSTALE   TARJETA POSTAL   POST KARTE. But there is no other inscription, nothing but the faded chop of the photographer's studio. You were a sales pitch, a hot tropical fantasy. The front of the postcard will always be the official public version of history. On the back, the personal constantly embattled one. In between, a razor that cuts everything from itself. You will remain in this plastic bag for a long time, propped up against the alarm clock in my room at Uncle's house. You will watch me sleeping and I will turn your face to the wall when I change my clothes. You will be the first image I wake up to, as I reach to turn off the alarm every morning. I will write nothing on the back of you. Nothing to challenge your meaning.

—Your uncle killed your grandmother. . . .
Ba would start telling the story until I yelled at him.
—I don't want to hear it.

A million stories surround her death. She starved to death in jail for anti-Japanese propaganda activities. She was shot in the jungles around Ipoh by the Japanese army as part of an offensive against the Communists there. She died of malnutrition because your great-grandmother withheld food from her, withheld it because she had said unkind things about her. She died of starvation because your grandfather, her husband, withheld food from her, withheld it because she was having an affair with another man. She was killed in a collision with a carrier transport on the Ring Road. A million stories. You know the name of each tear that falls in their telling. Each tear that stains the page. Indelible.

Your father. Auntie says it like it's coarse feed. *Fodder.*

—Your father. Last time, your father brings a woman with him, you know?

Auntie wrinkles her nose. Waves her hand in front of her as if to clear away a bad smell.

—*Ang mo,* she hisses.

Yes, I know her. Ba married a white woman in Los Angeles three years after Ma left him. She followed him back to Penang and then to Honolulu, leaving only the day he died. I hated the way she talked to me. Like I was a small animal. Or a child. She was always striking emphasis on meaningless words. And how are *you* today? But then I realized it was only because she had given up speaking to Ba. The only other life she could speak to were the small animals that inhabited their apartment in Honolulu. The place was overrun with cats. I counted at least sixteen of them. There was catfood all over the floors of their tiny apartment. I took to calling Ba's new wife *critter.* But only to Luk because Ma would never have understood and Ba would have slapped me upside my head if he heard that. Or maybe he wouldn't have gotten it either.

—When your father is here, he find a cat on the street you know.

He took it in.

—So dirty *lah.* But you know he kept it in the room. He lock the door.

The room you are sleeping in now. The room he had when he was here. The room with air-con. He left it in there all the time.

—We can hear it scratching at the door. But we are afraid to let it out because your father might kill us you know. He did that also many time. Once he take a knife from the kitchen and go after your uncle. Another time he say he is going to burn down the house. We don't hear the cat crying for our own lives.

After a few days, the crying stopped anyway.

—Your father say nothing about the cat.

Ba only wants to know where Uncle is. Where his money is. Then one day Auntie looked in the refrigerator.

—So dirty *lah*. The smell!

Ba had put the dead cat on the bottom shelf.

Another postcard. Greetings from. This time, the Penang Swimming Club. Lying by the pool. The important places the colonials built across this landscape were retreats like this: hill stations and swimming clubs. They could neither live with nor love the lands they conquered. The restaurant here is called the Snake Temple. The real temple it is named after is on the other side of the island. Here, the temple is overrun with the plump bodies of the local middle class. Barristers, bankers, executives. All attended by waiters and bartenders who know their names and desires on sight. *Hello, Mr. Lee. Gin and tonic, sir?* The bells of servility chime in smarmy chorus. The temple it is named after is a place overrun with pit vipers, seemingly intoxicated by the occasional smoky acts of puja. But most of the visitors to the real Snake Temple are tourists. They come to shudder at the sight of snakes winding their way up various images of the Buddha, consuming offerings left behind by a few unseen devotees. The temple is usually cast in shadows, its mossy walls overgrown with creepers and leaves. The sounds of the jungle reclaiming. Integrating. Syncretizing.

The forest is a place of incessant innovation. But in this postcard, its fringes are trimmed to merely frame the vistas of panoramic views. Snakes in temples. Snakes in swimming clubs. Exotic traditional dancing at casinos. Resorts. Fishing. Big-game hunting. Elephant rides. Adventure. It's all there on the front of the postcard. The caption on the back:

> *The national bourgeoisie organizes centers of rest and relaxation and pleasure resorts to meet the wishes of the Western bourgeoisie. Such activity is given the name of tourism, and for the occasion will be built up as a national industry.*
> —Frantz Fanon, *The Wretched of the Earth*

The ministers of the country play badminton with their former masters, returning after Independence for a few weeks in the sun. The government becomes an organizer of parties.

A middle class bereft of ideas keeps the bars, beaches, and brothels full of all kinds of flesh. In the northern reaches of Chiang Mai, an Australian pedophile is arrested. The newspapers carry a full supplement on the case and the horrors of child prostitution in the kingdom. The man hired two Hmong girls, one twelve and one eight years old. The police claim they found almost four hundred pornographic photos of various underage children with the Australian, a set of handcuffs, and a small knife that the man had used on one of the girls. The older girl said he made them take a bath before he began abusing them. The courts charged him with defaming the Buddhist religion, because he used images of the Buddha in his photographs. He was also charged with possession of pornography and a knife. Sexual abuse was not among the crimes of which the court eventually convicted him. During his trial, the Australian repeatedly claimed his innocence by insisting that he only took the pictures. The real guilty parties, he maintained, were those who developed them.

(image — commodity) — absence of narrative

I was wrong after all. There are no stories here. Only the images left from the stories. The stains on the mattress of history. The flow was not stemmed by the flash of the photographer's shutter, yet you have stayed behind. Stayed behind to see that the borders of your body are falling into place. Biological being. Medical statistic. Psychosexual construction. Civil entity. Legal identity. Thing. Even as your body becomes legible, the illegible Nyonya that you are is vanishing at the seams of the image. Your culture is a relic of antiquity. The only thing that remains is tradition. A dance without meaning. Keep this photograph. The sum of your blood quantum. Siamese, Teochew, Hokkien, Hakka, Acehnese, Tamil, Sinhalese, Portuguese. All those things inside you. You inside all those things. You. A matrix. Pregnant with inconsistencies and catastrophes, delusions and discoveries. Dreams of colliding worlds.

King Rubber

You're sitting on a rock in the sea with your cousin Ah Meng, casting for small silvery fish that lose themselves in the reflecting sun. Trying to retrieve a tangled line, you slice open your leg and now it's bleeding in the heat. You both ignore the red syrup trickling like embarrassment around your feet. It's so red it looks fake. Ah Meng catches small flat pomfret, one after the other. The bucket is filled with them. Later, the small bones of the fish will pierce your tongue as your teeth try to separate the flesh. The only fish you manage to catch is a small fat tiger fish. You feel like a real star, barely suppressing your confidence. Your cousin is excited and congratulates you as you try to dislodge the hook from its throat.

Back on the beach, sliding frozen shrimp over your hooks. A hotel casts its shadow on your back as you wade into the water and swing your lines as far as the tide will allow. The bait keeps disintegrating off your hook. Ah Meng is your height and not very handsome. Uncle doesn't know what to do with him. He's been out of school for a few months now, and he spends his days fishing. Occasionally, he'll help your uncle doing construction work, but it's never for more than a few hours at a time. Ba would have

beat a better work ethic into him. Ba. His brother. Your uncles.
Your birth certificate classifies them as *khek*. It means they are the
children of mercenaries and pirates. Passengers in every nation.
People who settle when they run out of prospects.

Ah Meng is far down the shore and you're fixing a new line.
A man wanders over from the part of the beach reserved for hotel
guests. He has dark-blond hair sticking out of a baseball cap, a
mustache, a wide, softening chest with dollar-sized nipples, and a
full, hard stomach rounded over bikini briefs. Even from this distance you can tell his hair is a toupee, but still he has a certain
pig-bottom charm. When he talks in English with a severe Dan-
ish halt, you smile back.

—What is it?

He asks slowly, loudly, pointing to the melting shrimp in
your hand.

—*Udang*.

You play along, fumbling for the English word. He guesses
it before you say it. Then, without pause or segue, he asks you to
rub suntan lotion on his back. Your cousin seems closer than he
was before. The man's flesh looks as pink as the rotting thing in
your hand. He's waiting for your answer.

You walk through the lobby of his hotel without a single
thought in your mind. No one challenges you as you take the
elevator up to his suite. He opens the door and ushers you inside
without a word. The air-conditioning is on full blast. You can
feel it pricking your skin, but when he runs his hands over you
he says you're hotter than a firecracker. He's dressed in his bikini
and a short-sleeved cotton shirt. He asks you to sit on the bed
patiently. He takes off his clothes, fishes around in his suitcase,

and comes up with a flat piece of black rubber. You wonder what it is, but before you can ask he slips it over his enormous ass. A pair of black rubber shorts that threaten to smother his erection. He smiles at you. You smile back and slip two of your fingers down the front of the shorts, pull them out, and let them snap back. He whimpers. You grope for multiple meanings behind his expression, but only one simple translation is possible.

He produces another piece of rubber. A shirt. And then another, that unfolds into a half mask, leaving his eyes staring out from an impenetrable flatness. There is a hardness missing from the rubber's surface. A lack that makes him look, somehow, more intelligent. Somehow, more inviting. But his new skin is too matte to the touch. It drags, tears at your flesh, and threatens to burn. You need to get it wet. You pull the shorts out again. Stick your limp penis down the front and breathe. Try to relax your body. When that doesn't work, you try to make your body disappear. Your flesh falls away, recedes into a red lacquer box, scarred by smooth drips running horizontally across its glazed sides. You watch the hinges close on you and calm your breath. On the fifth expulsion of air, you feel it start to trickle out and then stop. You start again, and this time a torrent of urine pushes out. He is surprised, but it only takes a moment before it fades into indignation. You put your hand over his mouth and continue urinating. You are surprised at how quickly your bladder fills his shorts. It starts dribbling out the legs of his shorts, coursing down his hairy calves. His eyes close. His breath stains your fingers, rude against your skin. You push him down, still peeing. Cover him with your body. The rubber takes on a new sheen. You feel his bones twisting underneath the thin membranes separating you. He turns on his side, so the two of you are facing each other. Run your hands over his chest, pulling at the elastic, clutching at the flesh underneath. You fall against him as if he were solid pavement, realizing too late that his body is not about armored plating but smooth clouds of slaughter. The meat hangs off the bone only slightly out of shape. Tired. A belly. A black stream crossing that belly covers you, implicates you in this little elastic web of violence. This was muscle once, you think, as surely as the cash-crop plantations around you were once a forest.

You insert a finger past his sphincter. It closes warm and wet around the first digit, and you dial it as if it were a telephone. But when you connect, it occurs to you that you do not know for whom to ask. You do not know his name. You open your mouth to ask, but the words get stuffed in your lungs. You bring your teeth against his chest, breathing deeply. Sweat. Piss. Latex. Deodorant. Swallow the whole earth. Drink the whole sea. He whimpers underneath you as your jaw grinds his two membranes against each other.

There is a pimple at the base of flesh separating his legs and he winces every time you brush it. You have learned to call this part of anatomy *taint*. Some queen somewhere lodged it in your vocabulary: *'Tain't ass and 'tain't dick*. But perhaps there is also the suggestion of spoilage and poison here. Following the discovery of the economic importance of rubber at the beginning of the century, South American leaf blight (*Microcyclus ulei*) became a much-feared disease because of its devastating effect on the rubber-producing plant *Hevea brasiliensis*. The disease is most conspicuous on the leaves. Infection results in repeated defoliation, dieback of the canopy, and death, even of mature trees. As the leaf hardens, the lesions lose their powdery appearance and become brownish, and the center may rot away. It is possible that the spread could have happened through attempts to grow rubber outside the natural range of the genus. Through attempts to expand production.

Context for homosas; in colonial capitalism

You spread your hand greedily across the seamless expanse of his backside. You notice what you did not see before: broken blood vessels, like fine hairs or brush strokes, crossing his ass. Railway lines. Capillaries without origin or destination. The remnants of some archaic verse. Your hand rises and then bears down with the force of frustration. You hear it crack across the room, bringing the desired effect. Grab him by the hair, pull him down off the bed. Make him crawl around the floor, as you undress. He licks at your calves as you expose them, but the effect is unsatisfying. His humiliation is merely perfunctory. You feel the urge to make it sublime.

Under colonial capitalism, industriousness was symbolized by the mule. The Malay unwillingness to expend labor on the plantations led to the characterization of the local population as lazy. The indentured coolies from abroad, however, earned the reputation of being "mules among nations." The laborers imported by coolie brokers in South China, Hong Kong, and Singapore were also called "piglets," and the people in charge of their lodging houses were called "heads of piglets."

Your fingers pull at his flesh, lifting muscle, cartilage, and skin from the bone. Probing. Exorcising his body, because evil always produces itself in the flesh. The master narrative of the original sin perpetuates itself in every shudder and twitch of our muscles. The wages of sin have bought the foundation for the ideology of exploitation. An ideology that could be the answer to all your problems, but it's not. Disillusioned, your hands return the flesh to his body. You search elsewhere, shoving four fingers in his mouth, pulling on his jaw. But in the end, you are just too lazy to rip it off his face. A conflict stirs in your gut. A conflict of belief. The conflict, essentially, is whether to accumulate or subsist. Whether to own the flesh you are touching or sim-

ply to pass through and over it, leaving it intact and alive. You
remember something vaguely, a rule of economic culture: A production system that is not mechanized does not build surplus.

A vibrator would be nice. You look around for something to
keep him full. Something low-maintenance. A cucumber. A dildo.
That would have required premeditation. Instead, you work with
what is available. A long-necked bottle of beer from the minibar.
A belt from his suitcase. A hand towel from the bathroom.

You truss him up like a pig. No. That's wrong. He looks
more like a package. His knees bleed into his chest until he is just
a lump of sweaty rubber and muscle, his face gurgling in the
scratchy triangle of your crotch. You grab him by the hair. Tie a
hand towel emblazoned with the hotel logo into a knot. Stuff the
knot in his mouth and tie the ends around his head. Lower his
face in tribute. Or in shame. You uncap the beer bottle and pour
its contents all over him. It slaps across the burning sea of his back,
erasing the drying white salt licks you left behind on the rubber.
Through his pleasure, he exhales. It is a wounded breath you hear
as you spread his ass apart with your hands and spit on his sphincter. There are a few encrusted hairs there. The crumbs seem almost unreal, as if they are too perfectly formed to have been
produced organically. His body becomes a thing underneath you.

Take a step out. Not far. Just enough to feel yourself falling.
Press the mouth of the empty bottle against his asshole. It puck-
ers, trembles, and then locks around the stem. You are surprised
at how smoothly it slides in. You marvel at how far it goes in.
The bottle might break. That is the reality of things. Bend a thing
back too far and it snaps. He shudders against the glass. You feel
your hand against it but can't tell if it's you or the glass that's trembling. You're all sticky with sweat. It's two hours later. He's lying
on his back, with his knees touching the sides of the bed by his

head. Remove the bottle. Play more closely with his fleshy ass, alternating your tongue with three well-greased fingers. You feel heat that was only suggested through glass. Power suggested only by the position of your hand at the axis of his body. He's trying to get his own dick in his mouth. Your suggestion. The tip of his tongue can barely touch the head. He says he's close, but you know he doesn't mean it in terms of space. He spends it all over his face, with his mouth wide open in disbelief. It's splattered all over his cheeks, and you help him clean up by wiping it into his mouth. He sucks on your fingers for a while and then, finally, you let him kiss you.

You're in the shower. He's sleeping. It's getting dark outside. Everything has a strange kind of sadness in this afternoon light. The air conditioner is singing over your head. He's snoring. The only changes in the room are two 50-ringgit notes underneath the lamp by the bed.

Musuh Dalam Selimut:
The Enemies
in the Blanket

From Fanon

Your skin is your uniform. A beacon and a membrane. Something to hold it all together. A uniform like dirt, but not close enough to earth. Dark, but not dark enough to hide your insides. Skin that betrays difference. Foreignness. Contagion. A pause. Usually a pause. Where are you from? The suspicion always cuts like a knife. Where do you want me to be from? The same question on both sides of the tropic. In smoky bars. In the light of day. I lie under the sun, hoping it will bake the answer into my skin. Bake my belonging. But it's not me that's lying back this afternoon, it's just my skin. There's comfort in that knowledge. Somewhere. Feel it lie back, flat and wordless, on the manicured lawns of the Botanical Gardens. A rainbow crosses the sky, half obscured from my view by a banyan tree. In the distance, black clouds roll over the channel, but here there is only diaphanous blue drawn across an empty sun. Still, the smell of rain is here, the smell of erratic violence and possibility. Skateboarders roll down the roads, dodging indignant macaques. White socks pulled high over brown legs. Icarus leaps toward the sun but the labyrinth still contains him.

A sign warns, in Malay, then English: JANGAN BERI MAKANAN KEPADA BINATANG-BINATANG. ALL ANIMALS ARE SAD AFTER FUCKING. WHICH ONE OF THESE HAS AIDS? But the macaques pay no attention, standing in the way of passersby, demanding to be fed. The same sign is posted at the zoo, in front of the orangutan's cage. There, the cage is empty. The ginger beast is absent. I remember him well, the joy he gave me, watching him as a child. The joy of looking. He would stare back at his captors. Bum cigarettes from them, his spidery arms snaking in and out of the cage. Subverting their demanding eyes by mimicking their behavior. He did everything but speak. He looked back at his audience with even cooler amusement than they could muster. He would sidle up to the front of the cage and look behind him, trying to figure out what fascinated the people outside the bars. I would always feel a weird kinship pass between the two of us.

A macaque chuckles, and I could swear he was looking right at me. Every laugh seems at my expense today. I want the ground to open and swallow the sun. Hide me. My laughable body. Touch the earth. Baked as warm as my skin. As warm as a dream with no beginning and no end.

The death of your father does not alleviate your spirits, as you thought it might. A messy death, his. To match his messy life. Bits and pieces scattered across continents. Penang. Honolulu. Los Angeles. New York. Bangkok. You linger in Honolulu for a few extra nights after the funeral. To put things in order. But there is really nothing to put in order. You sell his belongings easily to his neighbors. Spend your nights under the banyan tree in the park by the beach. Your eyes seem bigger at night. Extra alert. Drinking in every movement. The night becomes your skin. Pushing you along through the grass. A young skateboarder with a wool cap passes by. You catch his eye and hear the flicker of spit and contempt land on the gravel behind you.

Next, a marine rides by on a bicycle. Crew cut, flabby face. You lean back into the shadows of the banyan tree, those recesses where spirits still live. He turns around, slows down. Then, deliberately, jerks his head toward the public toilet in the distance. You inhale. Calm your heart. Play it off like nothing and follow him into the lighter shadows of the toilet. Inside, two urinals stand next to two flush-toilet stalls. Across from that, a mirror and a sink. He is standing at the sink when you arrive. You barely acknowledge him and step to the urinal. Feel his breath cover your neck. Hear the sound of your own water running. You are afraid to look at him. Afraid he will detect the black sea rushing through you. The quality of your skin. The quality of your heart. But your own desire suffocates your fear. You look over your shoulder fast enough to catch him checking you out in the mirror. Fast enough to catch him looking away.

You step around each other, never touching. Doing everything you can not to look in each other's eyes. You give him a little show. Warm yourself in your fist. Move your arms so there is no mistaking the intention of your gesture. Act like he is no longer watching, but you never forget he is always watching. You turn, without zipping up your pants. Barely look at him, and walk into the stall closer to him. Close the door until only a sliver of light comes through, slashing across your hip. Drop your pants. Peer through the crack of light at him. He turns to watch you, then adjourns to the stall next to you.

There is a small hole in the wall between the two stalls. Only large enough to extend a finger to the knuckle. You press your eye to the hole, transfixed, as he removes his shirt. Unbuckles his pants. His striptease interrupted by the banality of untying his shoelaces. He has a meaty body. Furry ass. A sunburn that has healed into a tan, except the area around his crotch and thighs still shines like a bandage.

Behind this wall you take turns looking at each other. Through the hole. Exhibited. Ownable. You stick your finger in the hole. He rests his penis on top of it. You bring it back out, a drop of moisture soaking into your skin. It is now possible to preserve sperm and eggs from animals in liquid nitrogen, forming a "frozen zoo." This would preserve the genetic lines of animals long after their death. It is now possible to preserve the image of a man in a file of language that can be transmitted by satellite upon request, forming a "cyber zoo." It is now possible, now at this hour of night, to possess anything you want.

So you go for it. You put a longer finger through the hole. Feel for something you want. Feel something warm close around it. Engulf you. You push farther. Until the wall scratches your knuckles. Hear him exhale behind the wall. You hook your finger up. Try to pull him back through the hole with your finger. But only your lonely digit comes sliding through. Bring it to your nose. Inhale deep, his violence into yours. Struggles for the monopoly of the spice trade.

You put your finger in your mouth. Feel it rub your tongue, that place where purity is a tasteless joke that everyone still enjoys. Your mouth shatters his body, dissolving his taste in your own sweet saliva. He sticks his own finger through the hole now. You bend to receive his sacrament. Open your mouth. Tame your oral cavity. Divide and conquer. He recognizes only part of your body. Only the boundaries. Only violence. Lips. Teeth. Gums.

There is never an adequate description of your body. It's illegible. Your body that does not love language. Your body for whom language is only contempt. An obstacle. A digression. You run your teeth around his finger. Secure it behind a dream of barbed wire. Under the Briggs Plan, the British evicted a million people from their homes and placed them behind double barbed-wire fences in "New Villages." Divide and conquer. Odor. Skin. Fingers. Fragments.

You return your eye to the hole in the wall. Watch the marine's matte body lost in the sound/noise ratio of your own ecstasy. You lean against the wall.

—Look at me, you whisper urgently.—Fuck. . . .

Arch your back. Tense your legs. Listen. The sound of gla-ciers eroding. Melting in the heat. You are disappearing. Your illegible body has finally vanished.

Full moon last night. I couldn't sleep. Every ten minutes I would get up and go to the bathroom in the dark. Try and find the hole in the floor to urinate in. Listen to the water make an arc in the night. Climb back into bed. Pull the pillow over my head and wait for the filaments of stories to run through. I waited to catch a ride on one of them. To wrap a dream around one of them and disappear into the night that surrounded me. Which story was it that carried me over? I can't remember. But when I woke up, I had a mosquito bite on my eyelid. Martina saw it first thing. She giggled. Called. Auntie came in to look at it. Auntie blushed and looked away, but Martina just kept on laughing.

—Must have been dreaming something sweet.

Another dream. It is 1948. You ride your bicycle up the dirt path to the plantation owner's office. It is midday in the dry season. The air is hot. You are cool. There is not a sign of life inside, but you know he is there. You walk assuredly into the plantation owner's office. He does not look surprised to see you. You bow at the waist. Smile. Say *Tabek tuan,* and then shoot him once in the head.

Someone else's dream. Graham Greene dreams he is in the bush, fighting the Malayan People's Liberation Army. It's the Emergency. They couldn't call it a war because Lloyd's of London wouldn't insure any of their losses. So they call it a little problem of security. A little internal problem that drags on for ten years and then several decades after that. In Greene's dream, little light-bulbs filled with gunpowder explode all around him. But he continutes to lead his men to victory. At night Graham Greene comes home to you. Sneaks into your bed while you're sleeping and slips his pierced tongue in your ear.

I gave Thong some money before I left. I'm guessing, but it's probably run out by now. He's probably gone back to Les Beaux to make some more cash. I could call him and ask, but what's the point? It's not like I can send him more money now. It's not like I can ask him to find something else to do with his free time. There are a hundred words to describe what he does. My favorite is *dek khai nam: a* boy who sells his water. I try to remember what those rivers feel like, pulsing under my fingers when we stay up late into the night, talking and touching each other. But every time the feeling comes to mind, it's eclipsed by a larger question. How can I love these flows that are rented by other men? How can I run my hands over them without wanting to own them myself?

Not really a dream. Your father's eyes always hold you in contempt, even in the photograph you have of him on his wedding day. Ma is putting the ring on his finger. Ba is staring straight into the camera lens. Straight at you. And even though you were not born yet, you can tell he is displeased with the outcome. In your dream, the picture is dying.

Fixed by father's gaze

Your problem. One interpretation: You look for guys like your father. Guys who can offer you the security your father was supposed to. But then, once they prove they can give you that security, you need to fuck them over.

Your problem. Another interpretation: You look for guys like the ones you're expected to. Guys who can offer you the security capital was supposed to. But then, once they prove they can give you that security, you become disgusted with it and need to fuck them over.

Both seem to blame narrator

I rise from the grass. The macaques scatter when I stretch my arms upward. Far above my head. Try to touch the sky. Exhale. For not having moved in the last hour, I feel strangely sore. All over. If my muscles ache, maybe it's from supporting the hardware of a million conflicts that never blossom into war: Israeli missiles, ADI space-based lasers, Nancy Reagan's face-lifts, W-53 thermonuclear warheads, MK 21 advanced ballistic missile reentry vehicles, NYPD bullets. From the drinks vendor, I buy an ice-cold *air laici* for 50 sen. I lean against the stand and sip it slowly. A little girl selling peanuts comes up to me. Looks at me quizzically and then points to my gold tooth.

—Hey, mister, that sure is pretty in your mouth.

After I sold Ba's belongings in Honolulu, I took the money and went to a jeweler on Mauna Kea Street. The only thing I could buy with the tiny sum I had was a gold grill for my tooth. The jeweler knew Ba. Cut me a discount. Engraved a dollar sign on it. No extra charge. *Because I know your father.* Every time I smile now: a little tombstone in my mouth.

Suck

Last night I dreamed that I drowned. My body filled with water and I became part of the ocean. I watched it like you do every morning when you come out to the beach for a swim. You watch it this morning. Wrinkling. Frothing. Breathing. Then you walk out into the water. Waist-deep. You stand there until the air on your back becomes unbearable and you stretch your arms out and dive in. There is not the crashing of waves but a lesser sound, a dull hum that tickles your ears, competing only with the beating of your heart. Hands dip into the ocean. Fingers tread uncertainly. The ocean turns black underneath your chest. You blow a prayer out into the water with your breath. A prayer that you don't touch anything rough and slimy. Anything with teeth. Then you feel the black waters hold you. Assure you. Remind you where you come from. Unseen hands pick you up and set you down gently. Unseen fingers of salt caress and sting you. You become a part of the uncertainty around you. Exhaling salt water. You feel it alive inside you. Awake.

Motions take the place of your body. Strokes for limbs, breath for organs, speed for skin. What is now your body slices across the ocean's tendons. A crest forms in the distance, traveling toward you. It gets taller as it approaches, and your head sinks into its warm nothingness. You topple. Cease your movements.

You remember your dream clearly now. The moment of panic as your mind separated itself from the truth of your presence and you fell beneath the surface. But this time you realize you have not stopped moving. The ocean itself is twisting you, jerking you like its puppet. You stay under as the wave rolls over your hair. Hug yourself in the warmth of the current. From on top the ocean looks like green glass. Dense. Fragile. Dangerous. But from underneath, it takes on another hue. A translucent blue, the color of perfect memory, pushing through your fingers, trying to go back from where it came. You look beneath. See ripples of the sand floor littered with starfish and broken glass and the skeleton of a notebook. Its pages skim the current like a school of fish. Fragments swim through your hair. The writing is still legible, bleeding across the lined pages. *She is not. Any more than the white man.* A flood of waterlogged confetti. *does not run straight away along the lines of nationalism. the pure products go crazy.* The words become a labyrinth. Its walls threaten to trap you, suffocate you. But in the name of love, you are given the ability to discard all manner of information. Stop. Exhale all your breath and then climb slowly up. Your head breaks the surface and your chest fills until it threatens to burst into flames.

Behind you, opaque black waves are capped with white. You pick a wave in the distance. The one that will carry you. Back. You watch it rise. Swell. Bear down close to you. Turn. Start paddling. Rise. Hear the quiet of the surf instead of your heart beating terror. Feel the dark surf hold you in it. A laugh empties your lungs of air. A laugh, inexplicable. A laugh that you feel confident on this tiny wave. Going nowhere fast. Your body seeking death like pigeons flying home.

The current snaps, finished with you. Your feet touch sand as I awake from the dream. My muscles sore. My body nesting in the sun. I run my hands over my salty face. Rehearse a language I am learning again. Words I forget as soon as I utter them. The words for eyes. Nose. Ears. Mouth. The journey south. Chest. Liver. The seat of passion. And, finally: heart. I listen for it to beat. Feel the skin drying on my bones. Feel the sun replacing the sea on my skin with oil and sweat. Feel the life inside me. Warming. Incubating. Consuming. There are a million viruses inside this body. *I* is just one of them.

I = one o' million viruses

Trace   Derrida?

One afternoon, Uncle takes off from work to take me to the cemetery. We each take turns washing up in the *mandi*. When he's done, I close the door behind me. Hang my sarong on a hook and pour a red plastic bucket of cold water over my body. Again and again. Until my flesh is cold. I comb my hair back, sharp. Put on my best white shirt and a pair of blue trousers. Just before I walk into a pair of suede shoes at the doorstep, Uncle calls from the car.

—Bring your camera.

Down past Wat Chayamangakalaram and the Burmese temple across the road from it. Past the Hindu temple at Waterfall Road. The car lurches up into the hills, swerving off the side of the narrow roads to avoid oncoming traffic. Then, through a gateway and down a long, impossible driveway. There is a house at the end of the drive. A red hibiscus tree is in full bloom, the blossoms shattered across the ground. Before the car stops, you see a tall boy, his face deformed into a mask of permanent laughter. It is the caretaker's adopted son, who can neither speak nor hear but communicates in some private sign language with his father. The caretaker recognizes me. He knew my grandfather well. I call him uncle, and he insists we come in to visit. The floors are well swept and the house smells of clean mold and boiling herbs. His daughter, <u>also deaf,</u> brings us steaming cups of milky sweet Milo. She sits watching us, smiling nervously.

—*Last time I remember your skin was very fair. Now you are as black as us.*

Uncle chimes in.

—It's the sun. All that wandering.

He notices my impatiently tapping leg. Insists on showing us where my grandfather is buried. But it's not my grandfather I've come to see. My grandmother is buried next to him. Their graves are backed into the side of the hill, like all the others. There is a shiny gray concentric stone marking the spot. It takes up the full head of the plot, reaches its arms around the earth where my grandparents are buried. An open embrace. Ba once told me when it would get really hot at night, he would climb into this same cemetery with his friends and sleep on the cool stones of other families.

There is no photo on this stone, like on the other ones. Another absence.

IN EVER–LOVING MEMORY OF LE ARN SAYNEEVONGSE

ALIAS MRS. KHOO SIEW HIN

DIED 1944

LEAVING BEHIND 2 SONS: KHOO ENG THENG, KHOO ENG TECK

IN EVER–LOVING MEMORY. But it could just as easily read PAID IN FULL. The image of a person can be used to merely establish identity and presence. To merely represent. As in, *This is a photo of the Grandmother.* The image reduced to the borders of the frame. The four sides of the snapshot reduced to a single point in history. Tell the story within the parameters of the narrative. Dare to stray from that path, with the memory next to your heart, and

133

it becomes impervious to time. Something history cannot acquire. A memory that cannot be destroyed. A memory that is not a possession.

She is the daughter of a Siamese father and a Nyonya mother. In marriage she will take my grandfather's family name, a Chinese name no one outside of this region can ever recognize as Chinese. My grandmother bears him two sons before she dies of starvation. The nutrients required have been harvested, packaged, and exported to the heart of the empire. The ground between us is crawling with thorny vines. Touch-me-nots. A dangerous root. Ah Mah's tombstone says only that she is the child of man and woman. We might be able to trace the line back to China. We might be able to recite the names that came from a village buried in the salt-fish mountains of the southeastern coast. But no one is interested in those kinds of roots. People here respect the dead. People here wouldn't dare to claim an ancestry that they did not prevent. Or to turn the past into an easy parable of the present. I run my hand over the bristle of *lallang* grass around the grave, listening for the sound it makes when it smacks the soft of my palm. The lullaby of a more sensual history. Not history inscribed on a stone, marked with the year of her death, 1944. The official reports blame her death on her frail physique. In the official version, individuals are responsible for their own deaths and no one else's. At the end of that story, there is only the individual. The official report relinquishes its own responsibility as easily as it absolves the sins of others. The biggest sin being that I did nothing to prevent her death.

The other graves are strewn with melted wax, ashes, burnt offerings. Food for the soul left by repentant children. A hungry ghost is a creature with a tiny mouth and an enormous belly, its physique fed by ambition based on craving, worry based on crav-

134

ing, disappointment based on craving. A hungry ghost has no heritage. If the children do not feed the ancestor, the children will be hungry their entire life and pass that hunger on to their own children. Inside.

For me, I am here at the end of a pilgrimage, knowing even as I bend my knees to the earth that there is nothing left to claim. There is no prepackage of identity or ethnic heritage left to possess. No folk tales passed on from Grandmother's knee. No warm flavors of home pathetically re-created on the other side of the planet. Nothing. Nothing but a hole in the ground.

I lay garlands around stone. Strike a match against a box and bring it to the incense before the rising wind blows it out. A match, not a lighter. Buddha cannot smell gas. Leave the candles and joss, upright burning embers. Fall to my knees. Bend to touch my forehead to the ground and open my hands as if to soften the fall. I do this three times. I whisper what I think is a prayer. It is the only prayer I know: *Anicca vata sankhara*. All things are impermanent. Come full circle.

—*Let me take a picture of you.*

Uncle arranges me next to the stone. Joss smoke scratches my skin. I watch Uncle's finger as it pushes down on the shutter. The last thing I see before my eyes spin shut from looking at it too long. I inhale air through a wall of teeth. My back tenses.

Hear the shutter open. Close. The camera's motor racing to the next frame. The camera getting smaller and smaller. Uncle's finger relaxing. His mouth open. Already. The sound of time eating its own children. The sound of my own catastrophe.

Bahasa Jiwa Bangsa:
The Native Tongues Have
Officially Been Reinstated

I guess I should be writing a postcard or something, but I've been enjoying speaking too much lately to commit pen to paper. It feels good to let my tongue go. To hit those high notes that would be mistaken for hysteria in other parts of the world. To make my voice bounce like rain in a monsoon barrel.

—Do you remember how to speak?

That is the first thing Auntie asked when I arrived. How could she have known that it is possible to forget such a thing? At Ba's dinner table it was forbidden to speak anything but English. The only dialect that came up off the table were the rumblings of Ba's prolonged headache in the United States. He would swear in Hokkien because he said it was the dirtiest language. Just saying hello sounded like a curse. *Chee la ka. Tsai tou kat. Chee la ka. Chee la.* Damn it all to hell. Damn everything.

English might not be as useful to curse in, but Ba said it was the key to everything in the world. Ba wanted us to master English because he thought there was a future there. Somewhere. When we tried to speak it at the table, though, Ba would fly into a rage when he couldn't keep up with what we were saying. So mostly we were just quiet at dinner. He seemed happy with this compromise. For a while, we thought we were doing it just to appease him. Ma, Luk, myself. For a while, we thought

136

we were making him happy. Making the silence that precedes every storm.

It is different here.

At Uncle's house, the storm has arrived. There is never a moment of silent repose. Every surface is dusted with life. Its sounds settle on skin, slowly working their way through the pores. It would take a minute to realize that the words that begin to inhabit the blood do not belong to one, two, or even three languages. It is not enough and too much to be bilingual in this house. You have to know many languages here. But you have to know the right pieces of them. The walls bounce with the sounds of the television. Video games. Machines in the front of the house. The sounds of technology become inseparable from those of animals. They circulate around us. Through us. We create one another. But these languages are not colorless like oxygen or ghosts. In this house, we are the dark-skinned children of the angel cast out of heaven. Speaking in the toothless tongues of the serpent of knowledge.

Every time I misunderstand a word I curse Ba. Curse him in the only Hokkien I have managed to retain. Curse him for making me forget the rest. *Chee la ka.* Breathe in. *Chee.* Breathe out. *La.* On the second breath you realize you are in fact a part of these conversations. *Ka.* You participate even if you don't speak. Even if you don't follow every word. There is no need to master anything here. Lie back. Get lazy.

—Eh, you.

Martina is sitting on the floor in the living room, pointing at me, reclined on a couch behind her.

—Lazy one.

I close my eyes.

—Come on.

She is playing Donkey Kong. There's a little console tucked suggestively between her legs that she stabs at with her fingers. The television screen in front of her is transformed into a battleground.

—Come play *lah*.

Squeals fill the household. A monkey climbs, falls. Hanuman rallying his troops in the service of King Rama. The circuits of war have already been programmed for understanding. Industrial speech never needs to be translated into vernacular. Those are the terms of development.

The game tires me. Auntie comes in from the garage on the corner and hands me an English newspaper. She can't read it, but she wants me to know what's going on in the world. I try reading Martina a story. Slipping back and forth from the newspaper's reportage to my own.

—It says that a schoolteacher from Singapore who was a member of the Communist Party is returning to Singapore. He was in the jungle for almost twenty years, fighting the government. Because China is more interested in fostering trade with its Asian neighbors, it is no longer trying to foment revolution. And because of that, Singapore doesn't think communism is a threat anymore. More than four hundred former Communist Party members have applied to return to Malaysia from their jungle camps in Thailand.

—Know what your problem is?

Martina does not pause from battling monkeys on the television before she prescribes the antidote.

—You don't know how to tell a story. Tell the whole story. From beginning to end. And don't leave anything out in between.

—Aiyah.

Auntie looks at her, almost horrified.

—Where are you going? Why all at once *ah?* Why so fast? No need *lah.* Tell the story like a broken mirror. In pieces.

—Cannot *lah.*

Martina exhales the cool breath of an angel.

—Too boring that one.

Auntie clicks her tongue.

—Aiyah. This one. Not yet twenty and so clever already.

Auntie turns to me. Sly.

—So, are you married yet?

—No, Auntie. Not yet.

—Good. Better that way. Travel. See more of the world.

Washing rice. The grains that fall down the drain resemble tears. You try to grab them up, thinking of your dead grandmother and the back of Ba's calloused hand.

You enter a language through a kitchen or a noodle stand. Then find yourself stranded there. The real language must lie beyond that.

They want to know what is going to happen to me. So we take the drive up to see a medium. A long ride up a winding hill. The sewage smells so strong, it's actually sweet. At the top of the hill is a wrinkled old woman working on a laptop. When the car pulls into her dusty courtyard, she puts away her laptop and greets us in Hokkien. Auntie and Martina switch from speaking among themselves in Teochew to Hokkien. I marvel at the control Auntie and Martina maintain over pitch and register. Try to remember how to make my voice carry a tone. The medium sends me outside to burn some joss papers in a tin drum. She goes inside the doorway and sits at her solid wood table and starts rapping on the top. From outside, I can hear her begin chanting. Conjuring the wind. I can barely follow the words that come bouncing out of her nose. The high whistle of invocation. The sound of rubies melting into blood. She is the apocalypse.

My dead grandmother is singing behind my closed eyelids. A high, expressive wail ending in my name. Her whispers caress the side of my face.

—Ah Mah, I think I've found a picture of you.

—*You're kind of clueless, aren't you?* Her tone is concerned.

What kind of spirit is this? There are more kinds of spirits than there are living folks these days, Auntie says. Every spirit is born out of the soul of a dead person. *Phi chua. The spirit of a departed member of the family. Instead of being reborn, she stays in the land of the living to protect her offspring.*

Grandma is wearing a high-necked blue shirt and black pants. The blue of her shirt is so deep and bright, waves threaten to form on it.

—*Mah knows you are doubtful. Mah has been watching you.*

I twist on my seat, wondering if she's seen me in action.

—Like, all the time?

The medium's body twists. Her arms knock on the table as if they were detached from her body, like the limbs of an insect that have been severed but still grope meaningfully for food.

—*I remember sitting for a photo. I forget when. Maybe I'm just imagining it.*

The camera was invented in 1839. It was one of those things, like railroads and cuckoo clocks, that it was thought would be useful in taking the nation into the next century. One of those things that would one day give us the knowledge of society and nature to put them both in order. One of those things that would, if not spare us subjugation, at least make us the first nation in Asia to have television and air-conditioned cinemas.

—*I think it was after I had met your grandfather, but before I married him. It was just before the Occupation. Your grandfather wanted something of me. In case we were ever separated. Something to show our children, he said. So they will know what kind of woman you are.*

The camera is not an eye. It records. And what it records is always a poor substitute for a caress. It can turn the body into a story. Elicit the same comfort as seeing a chart of the edge of the world or the passbook of a bank account. The camera can place us.

—*The photographer was handsome. He made me laugh a little, in spite of myself. He put me at ease. When he went to pose me, he touched my wrist.*

Ordinary men walk the ground without mindfulness. Not like the ghost of Le Arn Sayneevongse, aka Madame Khoo Siew Hin, aka Ah Mah, who always knows she is walking when she is walking. Knows she is breathing when she is breathing. Auntie says that, unlike Ah Mah's ghost, ordinary men are addicted to pleasure. We're always at the mercy of the senses. Enthralled by the eye, with objects that charm.

—*I remember trying not to look excited. I remember thinking if my children didn't know what I looked like, then I could be everywhere for them. On every face they saw. In every word. Every light. I tried to think of my body as something else. Somewhere else.*

Undoing the organism. Her body falls away. No more flesh. No more organs. Only a language that is a litany of scars. The calluses on her hips. The peeling sores across her palms. The deep unhealed lines crisscrossing her fingertips from mending fishing nets. The blackened teeth and reddened gums from chewing betel. The railroad tracks crossing her womb. The plan of the city tattooed like the crosshairs of an assassin's rifle on her heart.

—*And then, after he finished taking those photos of my body, he gave me the negatives and I burned them.*

—*All of them?*

—*Except one. I remember looking at that photo later. Thinking, Anyone could look at it. Anyone could see me. But what I was thinking, what I was feeling, no one would ever know.*

Ah Mah exhales. But what comes out of her mouth is colder than breath. As quickly as she appeared, Ah Mah is gone. There is no smoke. No mirrors left behind. Nothing vaguely resembling an image. Only an ocean splashed into tiny puddles by the foot of the medium, unwinding from her trance. That's the way she wanted it. Torn in pieces that never form a whole reflection. Like the aftermath of a racing car hurtling full speed into a school bus full of teenagers. Long after the blood was mopped up, I would never know where her body ended and mine began.

Satellite Woman

$\mathcal{T}$hen one day you decide it's finished. Just like that. Not an end, exactly, but one day you decide it's time to move on. You saw what you came to see. Did what you needed to do. So you call him. You call Thong, to make sure you are still in love with him. He tells you to come back. He says what you want to hear: *I miss you.* That is all you need. You bid farewell to Uncle and Auntie from the platform of the train station in Butterworth, thinking this is probably the last time you will see them again. You try to put some of Luk's money in Uncle's pocket, but he keeps on taking it out, putting it back in yours. Finally, he obliges and takes half of what you've been offering.

There is no open return ticket. No smiling cheongsam-clad hostesses and Ambassador Class seat on the national carrier. No porter, limo, and happy home waiting at the end of the rainbow. There is only a pleather seat on the night train back north, through what was once the most fertile part of the country. Twenty-six hours on this wheezing train. Twenty-six hours on a journey across the future. Twenty-six hours. Your head rolls back. Your lips part. Your eyes close. Saliva drools out the corner of your mouth. Your pores open, drink. Sun. Sleep. Dust. The slums built up along the tracks on the fringes of the city give way to a sparser panorama. Even the pretentious new two-story houses with satellite dishes built by farmers along the tracks still smell of poverty. The tracks that carry you out of the city are always parallel to open sewage. The sun that rises over the limestone shadows by the border also graces mountains of refuse: plastic bags, toilet paper, rotting parcels thrown from the windows of moving trains.

At Padang Besar, you disembark to clear customs and immigration. The Thai immigration officer looks over your blue passport suspiciously.

—*Can you speak Thai?*

You nod, weary but still respectful.

—*Can you eat sticky rice?*

—*Huh? Yes, of course.*

—*Som taam?*

—*Sure. Even nam prik num.*

The barest shadow of a smile crosses the young guard's face. He stamps your passport and hands it back without ceremony.

—*Then, welcome home.*

At Padang Besar, four young Dutch tourists stumble back onto the train to find a monk in one of their assigned seats. One of the tourists becomes enraged.

—Sir, sir . . .

She tries negotiating with the uncomprehending *bhikku.*

—We wanted four seats together. One, two, three, four.

She counts off the seats as if they were merely four more sufferings in a long list of inconveniences. *Tristes tropiques,* you think. *That's when it's hot and you don't get a tan.* The monk smiles. He takes his umbrella from the rack above his head and moves slowly, imperceptibly, to the dining car. The Dutch youths settle. They fish prepackaged food out of their backpacks, devouring the supermarket produce like famished children. When they finish, they laugh and toss the wrappers out the window. Plastic, paper, bits of food rain across the sewer's embankment, a trail that leads all the way to the border.

The features of the landscape begin to emerge from the brown edges of the forest a few hours later. There is only the slightest shadow to mark the place where the earth meets the sky. The ground is crawling with life. Women move between narrow trails, starting fires, turning chickens, roasting flesh. Men squat on benches over the rubbish, eating rice and fish sauce. In the engine's blur, the forms become indistinguishable. Garbage and life.

At Hat Yai, the first stop across the border, the police board the train with screwdrivers. They take apart the panels of the train, uncovering stashes of tinned asparagus, canned potato chips, bottles of whiskey. The train's porter looks on stoically.

At Hat Yai, the first stop across the border, women make their way through the cars with baskets of barbecued chicken and sticky rice on their heads. *Mee khao. Mee gai yang.* A young woman's call hangs in the air, her *ee* strangely uninflected and flat. Chicken breasts. Thighs. Legs. Wings. Feet. Heads. Innards. There is no part of the flesh that cannot be consumed. A young woman in a *Les Miserables* T-shirt passes by with a tray of mangoes balanced on her head. You call from your seat: *Ma-muang warn mai khrap?* And when she tells you they are very sweet, you realize she is a man. Satellite woman. In these dusty backwaters, that's what they call a drag queen. As if her identity could just be broadcast from outer space. As if her life were merely information, strands manipulated by a master molecule.

Under this fading sun, we are all just packages. DNA or Pringles. Waiting to be brought across the Thai–Malaysian border on the Smuggler's Special. Carriage wall panels filled with merchandise. Tins stashed in toilet tanks. Sacks of rice strapped to the bellies of women, passing for pregnant. At Hat Yai, children in ski caps and shorts wait for the train going in the opposite direction. They will leap on the southbound train just as it pulls out of the station. They will go as far as Padang Besar, smuggled across the border to cut down trees for Malaysian businesses. Their ski caps fold over copious quantities of speed they will take to keep up with the demand for their labor. Those same caps will hide cash on the journey back.

By the edge of the station, older women have set up their wares on wafer-thin sheets of cloth. Their baskets open like hungry mouths, still chewing their food. Warm and full. The baskets overflow with spiky rambutan, still clinging to their branches; memory chips cast off from factories in the Free Trade Zone; produce of the fertile land. One woman sits passively behind a wicker basket, lined with a plastic trash bag, filled with dusty rubber dildoes. It is the end of the workday, and at the junction where the train changes engines the whole station stands at attention when the national anthem comes blaring over the loudspeakers. The last song of the day. The train lurches out of the station on the final note. The sides of the track flutter with empty wrappers tossed out of windows. From a distance, they look like butterflies, stranded in the wind.

detritus o' commodification
littering routes o' travel

"Their salutations are decidedly peculiar. . . . They kiss with their noses, by pressing them against their friends', and saying 'Very fragrant, very fragrant!' while they take long, satisfied sniffs. Many are now learning to shake hands and make graceful bows like Europeans, but the imported kiss is not yet in vogue, and I do not see that it ever can be until betel is discarded, for at present the nose is a more kissable feature of the Siamese face than the mouth."

—"Siam: The Land of the White Elephant, as It Was and Is,"
compiled and arranged by George B. Bacon
(Charles Scribner's Sons, 1892)

Version

OK, OK, we know you're on a ferry. But this boat thing isn't working. Who takes boats these days? Forget that.

You're on the night train heading back north. The cities are a blur in the engine's path: Hat Yai, Phatthalung, Surat Thani. Discarded, incandescent stations glide by in a night black and elegant as heaven. An occasional blast of open sewage slams through the windows as the train wheezes into the silent pitch. In the second-class toilet, restless droplets of piss fall out the hole in the train floor, tumbling like diamonds on the tracks below.

Your body slides against the sweaty vinyl in defeat but you can barely sleep. You wake up at each full stop in the train's ascent, settling back only when your body feels the train heaving in motion. The rhythm of the creaking wheels reassures you. Progress. Conquest. Freedom.

The landscape is never the postcard. The body is never the advertisement. When the train pulls into the station, it looks so unfamiliar that you ask someone where you are. They laugh at your stupidity and give you the full name: the City of the Beautiful and Invincible Archangel. Or is it Invisible? Whatever. You're here. Again. You're surprised how unfamiliar the streets look from the taxi. Your bones ache from the train ride, your body begging to be unfolded. But instead of going back to Thong's father's house, you check into a small hotel in Pratunam. You want him to wonder where you are.

On your return, the city is empty. Flushed of life. On your return the city is a ruined and lonely place, a sloppy patchwork of unassimilable stories. The red carpet has been withdrawn, and you are just another aspect of the metropolitan crush. Once-friendly faces now stare at you, bewildered and offended. Threatened. You grit your teeth against the inevitable.

You spend two days without contacting him. You take special delight in getting drunk those two nights at the Milk Bar without him. You want him to know you can still have a life. You want him to show up at the bar and see you, a drink in your hand, a smile plastered on your face. You want him to be jealous. To not know what ground he's standing on.

The morning of New Year's Eve, you wake up in the early afternoon and call his house. You leave a message that you're back and will be at the Milk Bar that night. You spend the rest of the day lying in bed, watching television. You finally get up well after the sun has set and take a taxi to Patpong. Guns are going off in the distance, but otherwise the city is pretty much as it is every night. Pulsing. Unrepentant. Without resolutions. Champagne on the breath of everyone you kiss. It is 11 P.M. When next you check the time, it is well after midnight, well into the new year, and you are so high you can't even taste the whiskey in front of you. Thong walks in around closing time with three friends.

I had forgotten how beautiful he is. Up close I can see it clearly. How perfectly he is put together, all fluid lines, tight and endless. When he closes his eyes in rapture, it's easy to forget he is mortal. Easy to forget he is still alive. In his *Ten Books on Architecture*, Alberti defines beauty as "the harmony and concord of all the parts achieved in such a manner that nothing could be added or taken away or altered except for the worse." Beauty is something lovely, proper and innate, diffused throughout the whole. It is something daring you to enter it. Take it apart. Drown yourself in its disassembled pieces: bile, blood, shit.

You tell Thong about the hotel room in Pratunam. He doesn't say anything. He is standing next to you, leaning back into you, so you can wrap your arms around him, bury your head in the side of his neck. It smells of deodorant soap at first. All boy. But then you detect the odor of something else, like the inside of a mango peel. His body is burning warm inside his clothes.

He asks you if he can bring his friend Lek back to the hotel room with you. They're both too tired to go back home.

You're only a little surprised when both of them climb into bed with you and Thong starts making out with Lek. You're only a little more surprised at your initial reaction, turning over and ignoring them until the jealousy becomes so overbearable that you turn and face them. Move your lips to theirs, and dive into the fray.

At some point, you forget which, but at some point, you whisper in Thong's ear.

—*Let me get inside you.*

When you see this gets no response, you try again.

—*Or you get inside me. Whatever. I just want to feel you.*

It takes a few minutes for him to maneuver you so he can enter. It hurts less than you thought it would, but you don't make much noise, your mouth being muffled by Lek. When he gets inside, it's unbelievable. Not just that it feels so good, but that you can't believe he's actually managed to fit it inside. It's an uncompromising position, to be sure. But what do you care? You have enough plastic in your pocket to buy his whole fucking *muban*.

In the morning, you call the kitchen to bring up coffee. Leave it outside the door, you tell them. Thong is still sleeping, Lek is awake. The two of you manage a civilized conversation. You are able to avoid betraying your jealousy and you think, for a while, that the two of you might actually become friends.

Lek finishes his coffee, dresses, and gets ready to leave. He brushes his lips across Thong's sleeping cheek without waking him. You watch, slightly amused. Then he goes up to you, standing by the door, and leans over as if to kiss you on your cheek. Instead he whispers in your ear.

—*He doesn't love you. He loves your money.*

—Please.

You try not to look offended.

—What money?

Kreng Jai:
Fearful Heart

That evening I move back into his family's house. The walls seem familiar, even though I probably spent a total of two nights here before I left for Penang. His family seems even more familiar than Uncle's. But mostly, I spend the next three weeks around the house. I can't believe how uncomfortable it is here. How difficult it is to sleep at night. Thong takes to sleeping upstairs, leaving me alone in the basement. He says it's because his father asked him to sleep in another room from me. Some nights when I cannot sleep, I climb the creaky stairs up to Thong's room and stand outside the open door, trying to discern his shape in the dark. One night I was shocked when his sister emerged from the dark and closed the door in my face. The next morning, we pretended the incident had never happened. I'm the only one who seems disturbed by the new sleeping arrangements. Thong seems perfectly happy to sleep alone, without me.

I take a minibus and then a taxi into Patpong every few days to exchange the remaining traveler's checks from New York that I have stashed in my suitcase. Eventually, the daily exchange of dollars for baht comes to a slow grind. I accept every vestige of his family's hospitality, devouring it like I'm doing them a favor. There is never the mention of money, and for a moment, I forget who is paying for all my discomfort. I reason that I was never asked for money in the first place. Why should I dole it out now that I'm practically a member of the family? How can one put a price on something like this, anyway?

Thong gets more and more distant. He disappears from the house for hours without telling me. At first I play it off like it's nothing. Then, during the second week, I start asking him where he's going. He just smiles, shrugs.

—*Out.*

I ask him if he still loves me and his only response is that same smile: smug, assured, sexy. Sometimes he nods impatiently and I feel better. It's a rare feeling these days. There's little opportunity to feel much, though. Every time I try to touch him, he pulls my hand off, hissing something about his father. That's why Thong never gets demonstrative around me anymore. If it's over, he'll tell me.

One night, after dinner, I suggest going into Patpong to dance. Thong jumps at the idea. It feels like it's been forever since I've seen Luk or the Milk Bar. I always feel good walking into the Milk Bar with Thong, like I'm showing him off to all the jealous queens there. We find a taxi just outside the *muban*. The ride into the city is quiet. I manage to put my hand over his. He doesn't turn it over to assure mine, but he doesn't pull it away either. Someone, probably Muk, told me once that if someone desires, he listens. If he is desired, he speaks. I take our mutual silences as proof that we desire each other with the same passion.

The taxi stops at the mouth of Patpong. Reggae pulses from the open door of a car on Silom. A flood of tangled notes and disembodied vows. *Boom boom baby bye bye.* I smell myself sweating as we pass a table selling cheap cosmetics. Thong pulls me over and asks me to buy something. I laugh, that beauty could have insecurities about the shape of his eyebrows, but trot back dutifully and give the man some change for a black eye pencil. Thong is waiting where I left him. I deftly slide the thing in his pocket so no one else can see his vanity. That was cool, I tell myself. That was so cool the way I did that. Slipped it into his pocket so no one else could see. Our little secret. The two of us. To have a secret cements our love. It means that both of us trust each other. That there is equilibrium in our relationship. I treat him like a prostitute and he treats me like an equal.

I'm not surprised when he says that he doesn't like hanging out at the Milk Bar. All those stuck-up queens. Who can blame him? Those stuck-up queens defer to me, though. They offer me little bumps of coke as if to say *We love you,* and I, eager to hear the words again, from anyone, suck back those lines. They make me strong. Fearless. So fearless I don't even notice when Thong disappears without saying a word. I look around the Milk Bar and he's gone. Fuck it. I don't care anymore. I can find my way back by myself. He's probably gone home already, bored. But I'm not ready to go home yet.

I wander alone across Rama IV Road to the edge of Lumpini Park. There are two queens talking in the glimmer of the fountain.

—*Whatever we become, it's always our doing. No one else's.*

Weird. Sounds too much like a fortune cookie. It's ridiculous to think that all anyone becomes is their own responsibility. Surely other forces have had a hand in their making.

★ ★ ★

I make it back to Ladprao sometime in the early afternoon and fall asleep on the couch before the children come home from school. I dream that I am lining up to use an automated banking machine. This older man is in front of me. He is the kind of gray Caucasian authority you see on *Masterpiece Theatre*. He is letting me take cash, lots of it, out of the machine on his card. I suddenly feel the overwhelming urge to stick my tongue in his mouth. I suddenly feel thirsty.

Bump

You spend your nights by yourself now. A few nights Thong takes a taxi with you to the heart of the city, but he always manages to leave you there, so that each night you are alone. You try to forget that you are alone, try to immerse yourself in the currents of the Milk Bar. Try to make new friends. You and your new friends dump whole grams on the mirror and leisurely shape them into lines, sucking back gin and tonic. The trick, they tell you, is to admire how beautiful you look when you bend over and do your line.

You wake up one afternoon, your head still swimming. Unable to form sentences. How did you get here? The last thing you remember is being in the bathroom at Harry's, shoving coke up your nose. The last thing you remember is Muk in her vermilion rubber miniskirt, more of a Band-Aid really, with her hands on her hips.

When you manage to stagger up the stairs from your basement room, Thong is gone. No one in the house seems to know where he is. You hang around the house until around ten, then make your way to the Milk Bar. Muk looks surprised to see you. She's standing at a table outside the bar with O.

—Miss mess, you were so fucked up last night we didn't know what to do with you. We put you in a taxi, but you didn't know your address. You started yelling at the driver, *Just take me to Ladprao and ask anyone there where I live. They all know.*

—And that's not the K-hole, papa. That's for real.

During the day, his family is courteous to you. They offer food, ask after your health, but when you try and really talk to them they disappear. They busy themselves with other tasks. They are trying to avoid you. You never occupy the same rooms they do. Even your dinner is taken alone, seemingly after everyone else has eaten. Your only link to them is Thong, and he is absent. No one seems to know where he has gone, but his sister reports seeing him at home regularly, when you are not there.

When night is about to fall, your sorrow turns into anger. You can no longer stand being treated with his family's hungry generosity or his own cool amusement. You collect your things into bags. You want to leave him like he's left you. In the lurch. But then, perhaps you are being too hasty. A part of you considers returning with a taxi and leaving that night, without telling anybody. You go out to the Milk Bar for a second opinion.

When you finally get to the Milk Bar, it is nearly closing time and Muk is waiting outside with Luk.

—*Let's go, honey. You need to do some unwinding.*

Muk grabs your arm and saunters to the mouth of Soi Jaruwan, where a taxi is waiting. There's a party, after closing, at the brothel diagonally across the avenue from Wat Tadtong. A bunch of Milk Bar regulars are already there. There is K, a pudgy boy in expensive clothes who is vaguely related to the royal family and runs a S/M theme restaurant in Sukhumvit; Boi; Sulan; Sohn, Sulan's boyfriend; and six of the boys who work at the brothel.

The tables are piled with neat stacks of empty cigarette packages and cocaine. You roll sharp red 100-baht notes into straws and stick them up your noses, Hoovering up whole packages of the stuff in seconds. You wash it down with a flat gin and tonic, which almost takes away the taste of residue lingering in the place where your throat meets your nose.

You empty a cigarette of half its tobacco and its filter, then pour your line into it and stuff the tobacco back in. A million insurrections flow through your veins. You pack it like a pipe bomb. It sputters between your fingers, smoke crawling up your throat like dry ice. K is telling you about his plans for the fetish restaurant and expanding his clientele. You've never been there, but you've heard all about it. Diners are made to sit in uncomfortable high chairs. The food is served in dog bowls by abusive waiters in French maid uniforms and leather harnesses.

—It must be hard to find surly help here.

—Oh no. Not at all. You have no idea how easy it is to get them going.

He stops to rub his manicured face with what's left of the coke on the table and asks one of his two escorts for the evening to come and lick it off.

—Be bad.

K leans back. Sucks at his drink.

—Do something very bad. It's lonely here by myself.

Then, suddenly, K puts his hand to his mouth, as if he's just remembered something. He grabs your hand and pulls you, running to the bathroom. Two boys are leaning against a doorway on the way to the toilet. K drops to his knees before the toilet and starts retching. His body is heaving solidly under your hands as you rub his back.

—Don't you see what I'm trying to do? I'm not just a restaurateur. I'm trying to educate our people.

The boys, meanwhile, are distractedly checking you out in the bathroom mirror as they comb their hair. They throw you glances that lock you into belief. Belief that they're just doing this for a living, letting old men touch them. But you, you're different. Another dance ensues, a dance called consent, in which we move around each other. One dancer says, I want to believe you. And the other says, I want you to believe me.

Coasting, now. No money in pocket. So high you can't form words. In any language. The BMW is speeding down an empty highway at 4 A.M., the tires laughing on the road. Sulan's boyfriend is driving. She sits in front next to him, her eyes wide. She's only just returned from college in Geneva, where her parents thought she would keep out of trouble. But trouble seems to follow Sulan everywhere she goes.

—My Jaguar broke down last night on the superhighway. I was so scared.

Sulan says it like it means something. But she's just trying to fill the space between us. Then she picks up.

—The part I like best about doing drugs is the way your pores just swallow the tip of the needle.

Now we have something to talk about, sister.

In the end, you go back to your packed bags, your head congested with jealousy, cocaine, and tar. The sun has already come up. His maid opens the gate for you silently. She hates you. There is no mistaking her silence. She barely tolerates you, when you crawl in early in the morning like this. You apologize for waking her, and she barely smiles. You tell her you're hungry and she leads you dutifully to the kitchen in the back, separated from the rest of the house by a courtyard. She feeds you there in anger, as if you've betrayed her.

You ask her where Thong is and she laughs. It is a mean, tired laugh. You don't press her. You wonder where Thong is, whether he's inside the house, sleeping upstairs, or in some hotel room, sleeping in someone's arms. You eat a few grains of fried rice from a small plate she makes for you, but you have lost your hunger. You leave your plate at the table and adjourn to your basement room without saying a word. You lie on top of the bed, defeated, waiting for his father to get out of the bathroom so you can stick your fingers down your throat. All you can hear is his cough, splitting the morning.

All day long you hold the pillow. When you close your eyes it might be his chest you have your arms locked around. You won't let him go ever, you tease, but when you wake up your face is pushed into the mattress and the pillow is on the floor. When your eyes are open every noise belongs to him. The footsteps in the hall. A key turning in a lock. A motor idling. Your heart pounding in its coffin.

Step

Another day flies by with Thong nowhere in sight. You find yourself at the Milk Bar, early in the night, resting your head on the counter. Boi walks in, lets out a low moan of disapproval, and clicks his tongue.

—What's wrong, then? Sick in love, is it?

He drawls out each word in English, the end of each sentence curling up in a parody of a Swedish accent. Boi's last boyfriend took him there to live for three years before he got sick of the winters and came back home.

—Come on, *na*. Forget about it. Let's go *pai* Harry's.

Boi entwines his hand in yours as you walk down Silom like you belong to each other. Somewhere, maybe halfway, between the Milk Bar and Harry's, just after the twenty-four-hour 7-Eleven, you remember a restaurant Thong liked to frequent. Krua Silom is just down a narrow alley. Another part of the invisible city.

The first person you see inside is one of his friends, a sixteen-year-old girl with bristle for hair and a burning cigarette hanging from her full, moist face. She jerks her head at the two of you, unsmiling, and sucks back meaningfully on her cigarette. She's wearing a backwards baseball cap and a T-shirt that says *I may not go down in history but I will go down on your sister*. Then, at the end of the restaurant, you see him. He's sitting with an older man, who gets up the minute we sit down at a table across from them. He hands Thong something. Thong smirks self-consciously and doesn't say anything.

You used to like the fact that other men were having him. It made him more valuable to you. But now it's a value beyond your reach.

—*What's going on between you two?*

Thong laughs at Boi's directness. You could never be that forthright. You can't even speak the same language anymore.

—What's he saying?

You let Boi do the speaking. You let him relay the responses back to you in English.

—You always fight. It's no fun. But he's never felt this way about anyone before. He wants to keep you as a friend. He says you are always welcome as a guest in his home.

You can keep him as a friend. At least he'll give you that. You look at his hands and notice then that he is still wearing the ring you gave him.

You feel overcome with gratitude toward Boi. You press your palms together, lowering your eyes. You thank him profusely. You make it look like you wanted to hear this. *Thank you, thank you, thank you. I love you. You're like a brother to me.*

—Don't do that.

Boi looks away. Thong looks away. Even you would look away if you could, but you are too busy making a fool of yourself.

You make the final leg of the journey to Harry's with both of them that night. Three friends. Nothing more, nothing less. The bar is jumping. All the *off boys* who work at the brothel up-stairs are down here unwinding with a few very real-looking drag queens and some tourists. Two really unconvincing Lao drag queens are doing a floor show where they mock vogueing and trade ugly jokes.

—*What's the worst part of fucking an eight-year-old?*

—*I don't know, what?*

—*Having to kill him.*

You run into K at the line to the men's room. He looks much better than the last time you saw him, unloading in the brothel toilet.

—Still with that boy?

—Friends.

You step to the urinal and an attendant comes up behind you, places his hands on your shoulders, and starts pinching. It takes a few moments before you can adjust to the pressure on your muscles and let your water go. When it goes, a hard sigh comes out of your chest.

You fish in your pocket for a few baht and pass it on to the attendant, who smiles sincerely. K takes your arm and pulls you into a stall with him.

—It was the same with me, you know. When I came back from L.A. I didn't know anything either. Boys here are just like that. Fickle.

He offers you a small square of mirror with six neat lines on it.

—Better just forget about him.

Fractals of power race through your blood. You leave the stall with a newly profound sense of beauty and importance. The drag queens have finished their act and the DJ is spinning some anonymous Eurotrash house mix. Whatever. It gets the crowd moving. You look for Thong in the crush, expecting to be disappointed. But there he is, sitting with Boi, with a rum and Coke in his hand. You move toward him, but a hand gripping the inside of your elbow impedes you.

A skinny boy with incredibly damaged teeth looks at you as if he's just stepped from a car wreck. You grimace at him. He tightens the hold on your arm. His teeth are so jagged they could open canned sardines.

—*I love you.*

A small boy standing next to the Can-face Kid unleashes his hand from your arm.

—Sorry. He thought you were his boyfriend.

—Whatever.

You force a laugh and push through to Thong and Boi. You feel your footsteps getting louder and clumsier as you approach.

Thon is smiling that smug-ass smile of his. The one that makes you want to get on your knees and suck his dick.

—Whatever.

You call the waiter over. Order another round of drinks. Boi puts his hand over yours. Thong leans over and busses your cheek. As a friend. Nothing more, nothing less. You can smell the alcohol left in his wake. *Thank you,* you say to neither of them. *Thank you.* The waiter returns with your order. Rum and Coke. Gin and tonic. Seven and Seven. You count out your money and drop a fat tip for the waiter. The bills seem to fall out of your hand with no sense of time. Endless. *Thank you,* you yell above the staccato rhythm of the night. *Thank you.* You lose count of how much money you have put on his tray. *Thank you.* You lose track of how many times you have said *thank you* tonight when you really meant to say *I love you.*

★ ★ ★

A change in municipal administrations. There hasn't been enough time for everyone to get to know each other, so the law is in effect tonight. You're all at Harry's when the police come to shut the bar down. You sidle up to K.

—Come on. Your father is the chief of police. Can't you have a word with them?

He looks at you like he's already excused your stupidity several times today and wanders away. They close the bar, but not before K finds an escort for the evening: tall, mean-looking. You have the same taste in men, clearly. A group of you retreat to O's apartment.

O is keen on showing you his new Charles Jourdan shoes. You let out low murmurs of envy. He cuts you a few lines of blow, pleased with your flattery. You lean back, reassured that the party will never end.

So it's settled, you think, as you watch Thong, O's boyfriend, and K's escort playing poker. Just friends. Fine. A transition you can handle easily enough. You being an adult, after all. You, secretly expecting something like this, after all. Thong is getting fleeced quickly. But he's cheerful enough about it, as if he were high on his losses. He comes up to you and asks to borrow some money to get in the next game.

Fair enough. You hand over two hundred-baht notes. Not a lot, but enough to make you feel generous. Satisfied, you walk out to the 7-Eleven on Silom for a pack of cigarettes. When you queue up at the register to pay for them, you realize your wallet is empty. You run back to O's apartment and you freak.

First you see O. You ask him what to do.

—Just let it go. It's not a lot of money. Look, I'll give you what you need to get back home. Come on. Relax.

But you cannot be contained. Above the soft murmurs of the poker table, you hurl your own challenge.

—What's my name, Thong? What's my name? Did you forget my name? Is my name Lotto? Then why are you trying to play me, bitch? Why did you steal my money, you fucking whore?

Your redundancy bores him. He smiles at you and tells you he's your friend forever. Then he leaves, without readjusting his smile. You follow, but by the time you're on the street he's already in a taxi whizzing down Silom.

I go home and he is sleeping in bed. Alone. Without undressing, I lie on the bed next to him, careful not to wake him. I can smell him. I want to reach out and touch him, but he's already told me in so many words not to ever do that again.

Siam Sanuk Khao:
Bitch Dub

A fly wakes me up just three hours after I've managed to fall asleep. A fly exiting from the crease between my face and the pillow, singing like a fading alarm. (Thong's father once caught me sleeping with the pillow between my legs and nearly had a heart attack. "No good," he sputtered in English, suddenly concerned with propriety. "Thailand . . . head." I wish people here would stop trying to teach me the fine points of my own fucking culture, you know?) I watch the fly dance a minor arc around my arm before it gets bored and wanders out of sight. Thong is nowhere to be seen. I lie there, trying to piece back the night before, wondering when it was that Thong left this room, but I can't remember. When I finally get out of bed, I wander around the first floor looking for someone else. I look up the stairs to the second and third floors, where everyone else sleeps, but don't go up them. Then I go out to the kitchen and look for the maid, who looks up for a moment from scouring the breakfast dishes to barely acknowledge my entrance.

—Coffee?

She ignores me, bends her head toward the faucet.

—*Ga-fei,* I try.

She continues scrubbing the pans.

—OK then, *nam cha.*

Then I notice the pot of coffee in the corner and grab a cup and try to pour it, but she suddenly gets concerned that I'm serving myself and comes over and pours it for me. I sit at the kitchen table and wince, looking at the clock, wondering why I wasted three whole hours in bed. I shower, get dressed quickly, go out to the road outside the house, and wait on the curb for either a taxi or a minibus to come by. I smoke a cigarette, watch a dog wander up the street, a motorcycle zoom by, and finally the bus come slowly up the street. I get up, wave to the driver as if I know him, climb in the back without saying a word, and take my place next to a young girl who tries hard not to look at me. The bus makes a few more stops before finally landing by Vibhavadee Rangsit. I give the guy in the driver's seat 10 baht and walk to the taxi stand before he can say anything. There's a cab waiting for me. I ask the driver how much the fare is to Silom, tell him it's too much money, try again, and finally settle on something like 15 baht less than what he asked. The ride to Silom is not uncomfortable and surprisingly fast. I get the feeling as we speed down the highway that I'm going the wrong way, that perhaps this ride is too easy because we should be going the other way, like everyone else, but no, in no time at all he turns down past Lumpini Park and I'm telling him where to stop.

—*Jawt thi ni.*

I pay him, thank him, and get out, walk past the bars, all closed up, that I was just in six hours ago, and go to the bookstore. I look through the cookbook section and then the magazines and then the guidebooks and settle on a backpacker's guide to Kampuchea because last night Boi showed me a belt someone bought him in Phnom Penh that had a rough buckle hammered into the shape of a Khmer angel that I really wanted to buy but Boi said he had never seen them on sale in Bangkok. I put the guidebook inside a copy of the *Bangkok Post* and go to the counter and pay for the newspaper. I walk out across Patpong, and a girl runs out of a bar wild-eyed and grabs my crotch. She screams.

—*You are cute!*

Then she runs back to her friends outside the bar, who are laughing really hard now. I ignore her, readjust my sunglasses, walk up the driveway of the Montien, passing the *sala phra phum,* ignore it, walk up to the doorman, smile weakly. He opens the door for me and I walk past the security guards like I live there, take the elevator to the second floor, and walk out into the sun by the pool, empty at three in the afternoon. A terrible hour of the day, I think, and wave to a pool attendant who is clearly on break. He gets up slowly, walks over, and when he's close enough to whisper to, I ask for a freshly squeezed orange juice with gin. He turns and I strip down to my underwear.

—Oh, and a beach towel!

He is only slightly startled by my yell. I sit on the edge of the beach chair until he comes back with a towel, sign the bill with a room number that I had when I once stayed at a hotel in Paris, and go through the newspaper. It's been a while since I've read anything besides Thong.

Thai Airways applied to buy 21 new Airbus and Boeing aircraft over five years, for 125 billion baht; it will sell 31 to help pay. The British heroin smuggler Sandra Gregory received a 25-year prison sentence in her two-year-old case. Accused drug smuggler and ex-MP Thanong Siri-preechapong applied for bail of $900,000 from the Los Angeles court where he will be tried; US prosecutors objected he might flee with his other $160 million. The former monk Vinai (Phra Yantra) La-ongsuwan applied for a U.S. work permit; the government had once vowed to ask for his extradition.

Harvard University researchers discovered that Type E HIV, found in Thailand, survives in the reproductive tract better than other types; this accounts for the heterosexual nature of the disease. Malaysia appeared for the first time on a U.S. list of countries where drug trafficking and money laundering occurs, and was unamused. Lee Kuan Yew, who often tacks against the wind, supported French nuclear tests and said China stands to gain in a protracted effort to reunify with Taiwan. China warned it would retaliate against any U.S. trade sanctions. A firebomb hurled into a Taiwan karaoke bar killed 13 in Taichung. Chinese government astronomers named a newly found planet after one of their richest citizens. Three French tourists died in a Phnom Penh boating accident on the Mekong. Oscar-winning real-life Killing Fields survivor and humanitarian Haing Ngor was shot to death in Los Angeles. Filipinos celebrated the tenth anniversary of overthrowing Ferdinand Marcos; his wife, Imelda, led a prayer for Swiss bankers. The luxury Cunard liner *Sagafjord* foundered off the Philippines. Chun Doo Hwan told the court the millions he received when president of South Korea weren't bribes but donations.

Hamas bombers killed 27 Israelis in two attacks; Israel told Yasser Arafat to crack down on the militants—now!—and he bent to the task; Syria-Israel peace talks continued. The United States said Libya is nearing completion of a new chemical weapons factory, largely built by Thai contractors.

France set up another new organization to protect the country against foreign influences. France honored Tina Turner for her wonderful singing. France announced plans to rebuild the military in a more American style. World junior flyweight champion Saman Sorjaturong stopped Mexico's Antonio Perez in the fourth round of their WBC title bout at Chachoengsao.

A special supplement on doing business in Indochina catches my eye. The greed spilling through the type is poetry.

Where the oil and gas could be
Where offshore oil already exists
Close to the border finds
SPECIAL FEATURE
BIG BEAR
Production forecasts rocket
As seen from Sydney
As seen from Kuala Lumpur
As seen from Tokyo
Mitterrand and the Total Factor
Hanoi unveils strategy for '90s
Industry delegation at June London conference
NEWS FROM THE OIL FIELDS
Vietsovpetro forecasts 6.3m tonnes for 1990
SEISMIC LISTENING POSTS
Hanoi government plays cards close to chest
HANOI BEAT
IMF opens permanent office
ANZ bank opens office

THE ECONOMY
Cooperation not conflict
INFOEXCHANGE

Before I know it, I'm finishing my second gin and juice. I get up, dip my toe in the pool for the first time today, and think it is too cold to go swimming, even though it's probably a wet 70 degrees in there. I pull on my clothes and walk out the hotel into Surawong. It feels like forever before I finally get to Lumpini Park. They've turned up the national anthem because it's that time of day, and everyone stops in their tracks until it's over. Even me. Still playing at belonging. When it's finished, I buy a bottle of drinking water and go walking farther into the park until I notice someone has started following me.

You'd be surprised what trouble folks can get up to in the bushes of Lumpini Park this early in the evening. I'm surprised myself. Shocked, really, that no one can see what's going on here. Some burly Lao guy has his black dick stretching the mouth of some little light-skinned queen on his knees in the grass. I don't notice at first, but actually there are two queens on their knees in front of this guy. That's how hot he is. The guy that's followed me into this clump of bushes runs his hands under my shirt, starts licking at my chest, then drops to his knees with a thud. He tries to give me head, but I can't get it up. I'm too transfixed with the sight of this guy in front of me getting serviced. I can smell him from here. He smells like an airplane. Lingering taste of nicotine, wool, and cabin-class Bordeaux. The man on his knees in front of me has vanished; in his place is a cold pool I sink into again and again. The queens working on the meat across from me are really getting into it. If they could swallow this man, I know they would. But he makes no move, just stands there, his arms behind his back, his hard chest sticking forward under a thin green T-shirt. We regard each other with the skeptical detachment of consumers in Foodland. Under this sky, we are neither hetero- nor homosexual. We are just smart shoppers. As if he could feel the exchange, one of the queens looks up to see what is holding the gaze of his man. He turns to look at me, without letting the rubbery dick in his mouth drop from his lips. A tear starts to roll out of his eye. Before it drops, I give the man in front of me a light push on his shoulders, button up my fly, and walk out the park, past the monument to black Rama the modernizer, past the rush-hour traffic at a standstill on the road named after him. I see a Mercedes-Benz with a bumper sticker that says MY OTHER CAR IS A . . . PENIS and walk up Rajdamri to the Erawan shrine, dip my head and bring my palms together like I live here, wait for ten minutes until it looks like I won't get killed by crossing the inter-section, and run across to the World Trade Center. It will be a few years before they finish this, one of the biggest shopping malls in the city. More upscale than Mahbunkrong. That's the plan, anyway. I sit on the cold marble steps of the site, watching the traffic slow, the sun set, the streets choke. I feel like sleeping for the first time in days. Weeks. Years. My skin feels as empty as my wallet was last night. Thong didn't steal my money, but it feels like he's taken something more. I think of catching a taxi back to Ladprao, lying down on a bed next to him, and shutting my eyes. Just the proximity would be enough to put me to sleep like a baby. But the evening traffic jam has just started. The party's just about to begin.

Nonstop Live Show

Non Stop Live Show. No Entrance Fee. No Cover Charge. Pay only for drink. Beer 50 baht. Whisky 55 baht. Kloster 55 baht. The Show Programme for this Night. Pussy Pingpongball. Pussy Shoot Banana. Pussy Smoke Cigarettes. Pussy WriteLetter. Lesbian Show. Boy and Girl Fucking Show. Beer Bottlepoker Pussy Open Beer Bottle. Pussy Pick the Desert With Chopsticks. BigDildo Show. Fire Stick in Pussy Show. Razor Thrilling Show. Flower Hanging Show. Whistle Blowing Show. Horn Blowing Show. Bottle Cracking Show. Pussy Irrigation Show. Fish Push Insideher. Egg Push In Tohercunt. Can dle show. Oral Sex and Sex 69 Show. Long-Eggplant Push Into Her Cunt. Pussy Drink Water Bottle Show. Blue Movies Film Too.

Gas the House and
Light the Building

On the eve of martial law, our attention is diverted to the plight of the individual. Stranded with a blue passport in a sea of expendability. The television news and game shows reduce the turn in history to one of those unfortunate events that catches a few civilians in the crossfire. Upstanding members of the business community. Some college students. A few foreign nationals. That sort of thing. There are the usual protests lodged with the usual ministries. The usual rush to board the next departing flight. The usual reassurances that the change in power will not affect productivity. Efficiency. The price of a line in the toilet at Harry's. A quick massage at the urinals. In our language, coup d'état means business as usual. It would have been impossible to predict the exact moment the military decided to overthrow a few corrupt and superficial years of "civilian" rule. But then, it would have been impossible to deny the inevitability of the moment. Everyone knew. Even you. Everyone knew the military would never stand for competition in the business of corruption.

On one of those nights before the tanks took up their position at the crossroads, you go out like it is any other night. You stay out until well after you know you are not going home with anybody. At least not for free anyway. You walk careless down Silom, too coked up to be spinning from the evening's liquor.

Walk past pop songs suddenly pregnant with meaning. Walk into the all-night Patpong pharmacy and ask for a dozen Percodans. Just enough to keep your teeth from grinding together. He remembers you from the night before and refuses to sell them. You moan. Plead. Say something about a toothache when it's really your body's ventricles that need quieting. You switch to English and insist. He lets you buy three, and you gobble them up without water the minute you're outside the shop. A couple you know who perform live sex shows on Patpong see you in the street, weaving your way back to Silom. You fully intend to walk the hour-long drive to Ladprao. The couple calls to you.

She is sitting on his lap, and when you get closer you see that she is handcuffed, discreetly, to the chair he is sitting on. They laugh about it. He asks if you want to buy the key. You think it over for a second and then agree on condition that he come along. He doesn't even answer. Just unlocks the cuff around the chair and handcuffs her to you.

The hotel receptionist barely looks at you when you fling down your credit card to check in.

—A suite for three, please.

You say it like you are somebody, refusing to answer her when she asks in Thai what kind of room you want. The hand-cuffed girl just keeps on giggling and pulling away from you. Her husband follows behind and you look at him, wondering how someone who can perform live sex acts in front of a nightclub audience could suddenly seem so timid in a hotel lobby confronted by the imaginary gaze of disapproving bellhops and off-duty maids.

A key opens the flimsy wooden door to the cell. The mattress is stripped of bedding. The three of you stand there for a while, awkwardly trying to figure out the decorum of the situation. Then you all remove your shoes and sit down on the bed.

She is the first to lie back, still handcuffed to you. You look at her, trying to take off her clothes, and then bum a cigarette from her husband. He chuckles, hands you a cigarette, lights it for you, then uncuffs you from her. You feel the smoke curl into your lungs. Light your head on fire. Nourished, you motion for him to join her.

You watch him take off his clothes, down to his sleazy red bikini underwear. You let out a low wolf whistle. His wife laughs, snickers something unintelligible about you, and then pulls him close to her. You watch them writhe on the dingy mattress. Watch him roll her left nipple between his teeth, his hands barely moving across her body. After a while, you forget they are having sex, they are so calm, nearly motionless. It isn't until you readjust yourself that you see he has actually penetrated her.

That sort of thing.

She looks at you over her husband's back. Smiles and motions for you to get close to him. You lie down beside him, still clothed, running your cold hands over their bodies. Trying to figure out where one body ends and another begins. Feel their genitals, as warm as yours feel distant. You brush your lips against the back of his neck. He is oblivious to you, barely turns around. She smiles dreamily at you but couldn't care less if you are there or watching TV.

You get back up, start to take off your clothes. Feel a flush the minute you unbutton your shirt. The blood trickling through your veins becomes air. No. Lighter than air. Nitrogen. Your body threatens to float away in a sudden burst of flames. You crawl to the bathroom. Try to vomit. Nothing comes out. You sit on the toilet. Feel the sweat gather in your armpits and run down your ribs. Hear yourself whimper. Put your head between your legs. That feels a little better. You grow impatient in this position. Try to raise your head, then your body. You stand up. Your knees start shaking. You see the shipwreck of blood on the inside of your eyelids. And then, just as suddenly, you see that ocean drain of color. Your eyes wrap around something sweet and white. You feel your cheek cutting through space to touch the floor. When you open your eyes again, you see how carefully the tiles of the bathroom have been cleaned by the maids you passed in the lobby. There is not a single speck of dirt in the grout that lines the bathtub. No wonder they were so arrogant.

You raise yourself up, look in the mirror. Wipe a streak of blood from the corner of your mouth and smile at yourself. Smile at how good you feel. How numb. When you finally emerge from the bathroom, you see that your two companions have fallen asleep. The sun has come up. You draw the blinds.

As the light outside becomes impossible to ignore, you watch her glow in her shackles. Even as they cut her wrist. There is blood on the pillow. But you aren't sure if it is yours or hers. The only thing you can be certain of is that it is the blood neither of a civilian nor a general. You watch two flies start dancing in a line around her wrists. Try to fall asleep in their arms. Feel their warmth becoming more and more vague. Touch a damp red spot on the pillow as it diffuses into brown. A bolt of sunlight sneaks through the curtains, laying itself across her pubic hair. Flax transforms to gold around her vagina. But the alchemy is all wrong this morning. You wonder at how unsatisfied you feel. How these arms around you are so clearly the wrong arms. Arms capable of only the stingiest embrace.

You rise with greater clarity. Feel your muscles twitch with purpose, knowing you will never fall asleep again. You make it to the shower without falling down. Spend a long time under cold jets of water before, assuring yourself that you are really sober, you dry off and put on your old clothes. Leave them sleeping on the undressed bed. Scratch the back of your greasy neck. Look at your reflection in the elevator door. See what could still be considered youth squinting back. Walk out the hotel lobby without turning back. You put a 100-baht note in the first tin cup you see rattling on the sidewalk. Just to hear the hand holding it call you brother.

slip

Your mistake was letting him out of your sight. Now he's vanished. Without a trace. You heard things like that happen all the time. But you never thought it would happen to you. The word for hello can also be the word for goodbye.

—Where's Thong?

The maid shrugs.

—Bitch, I asked you a question.

She walks away smiling.

—We're a bit worried about you, love.

Luk rings you in the afternoon at Thong's house. You nearly rip the phone from the maid's hand. You try hard to suppress a smile. It's a proud smile. Proud that you know someone well enough that they would call you here. That you know someone else in this city besides yourself.

—O said you lost it the other night.

—Was he appalled?

—No, of course not.

Liar.

—Listen. I want you to get out of there. I don't even know why you're staying there anymore. Come stay at my place. I'm going away this weekend. You can have it all to yourself. There are a few problems with the hotel upcountry. Apparently, the owners have added on an extra wing without consulting us. I'll be gone until Monday. But Boi and Muk will take care of you.

Luk's apartment is pretty much what you'd expect an architect's apartment to look like. Pristine. Even the mess has an intellectual clarity to it. His firm offered him a house in Ramkhamhaeng, but he told them he'd rather live in the heart of the city. Or in one of its hearts. The city is a monster with many hearts, connected by fragile, clotted arteries. Luk settled for a furnished apartment in Sukhumvit. I stop off at the pharmacy on the street for a few Percodans. Just to soothe my nerves. Then I take the elevator up to the penthouse. There's not much of a view. The sprawl is so wide in this city that it's hard to figure out where the skyline begins. There's an envelope with my name on it sitting on the kitchen table. Inside are ten U.S. $100 bills. Really. Luk can be so sweet sometimes.

I flip through my brother's CD collection. It's hard to believe how bad his taste in music is, but there's a few choice joints in here. I settle on Art Blakey, pour myself a glass of water from a bottle in the refrigerator, and wash down a Percodan. I hit his bed, hoping to catch some sleep before night. But instead, I watch the windows in the building under construction across the way. They fill up with workers, mortaring bricks, punching in window frames, reinforcing beams. They are oblivious to my stare. There is something beautiful and untouchable about their labor, something apparent only to me. Because I'm the only one who can take a step back and look at what they're doing. I'm the only one, I think. I'm the only one who can tell them how beautiful they really are.

Boi and Muk take me back to the brothel near Wat Tadtong. I want to forget about Thong.

—The manager thinks you're cute.

Muk cups her hand to my ear, as if the secret is so luscious it will spill over.

—He doesn't have to sleep with anybody, but he wants you. You like him? A gift from me.

—No, no, let me pay for this; you're too generous.

Muk waves me away and calls the manager over.

Why did I do so much coke last night? Even without saying it, this is a stupid question, floating around in my head sometime after noon when I finally regain consciousness. Sort of. Why did I do so much last night? Even after the manager sat down next to me and ran his hands all over mine. Even after he told me how beautiful I was. Even after I didn't need the confidence or the conversational skills. Even after I had won my prize. My skin is red and in some kind of a major rebellion, shedding snowflakes on an oily pillow. I don't know who booked me into this hotel room. It has all the pretense of a five-star hotel. Twenty-four-hour room service. Clean sheets. Complimentary soap. But it has no windows. More like a cell than a room, really.

Shit.

My finger traces a sting on my chest. Near my heart. There's a rough scab forming around my nipples. Sex was a disaster. I couldn't get it up. That much I remember. I asked him to bite me, hoping that would bring me around. But it was useless. Soft and useless. He's in the shower. I'm poking at a tray of food I don't even remember ordering from room service. I start to devour a plate of cold squid and rice as if it is the only food I've ever seen. He comes out and makes a face. Self-conscious, I leave half the plate untouched. I almost forget to give him his tip. When I do hand it over, I clumsily ask him if he wants to spend the day together. He has other plans.

Hard Candy
(Chocolate Thai)

A gram later and I'm finally able to convince myself that the rash on my forehead isn't as bad as I thought it was and I can leave the hotel. The woman at the front desk asks me if she can call a taxi for me but I ignore her and walk out front where all the taxi drivers are sitting around and smoking and probably talking about the good old days, when the cabs were driven by Chinks and they could stay at home and drink beer instead of having to work all the time. I go up to one who has no nose. Don't ask. He just doesn't have a nose. That little flat bump that everyone else has in the middle of their face is shaved smooth, but he's pretty good-looking otherwise. I tell him where I want to go, my complete mispronunciation of the place confusing him badly. Then I pull out the card with the address of Les Beaux and he gets it. He repeats the name of the place, this time with all the tones in the right places, and says he knows it. I ask him how much and he names some ridiculous price, three times as much as it would cost me if I took a cab down the street. I tell him that and he cuts the price in half. Still too expensive, if you ask me, but I have at least half of Luk's money left. And I'm worth it after all.

When you get to the bar, the manager looks confused to see you.

—Where's Thong?

—No idea. Haven't seen him since you were last here.

You look up. Projected on the wall, there's a slide of some little kid, sixteen tops, who looks really unhappy but has a not unattractive organ, posing with some really cheap-looking tribal jewelry.

—How are you doing?

You hope there is no trace of sarcasm in your voice.

—It's my last night here.

You raise your eyebrows at the bartender and he comes over and bows his head.

—I'm going up north. To be ordained.

—Gin and tonic, please.

You fish in your pockets for the pink parcel of coke. Instead, you find a lonely Quaalude. Before bringing it to your mouth, you manage:

—Look, I really need to see Thong. If you see him, tell him I really need to see him. OK?

He doesn't answer. Just smiles. Maybe the smile is a little too smug. Whatever. It leaves you both quiet for a long time. When the bartender sets your drink down you pick it up almost immediately and finish half of it. You don't know what the manager is doing because you can't bring yourself to look at him anymore.

Three Australian tourists walk into the bar. Nobody seems particularly surprised to see them. Nobody, that is, except you. You thought this place was exclusive. The manager excuses himself, goes over, and makes them feel at home. They are kind of handsome. In a sunburned way. You notice one of them is staring at you. You feel the blood, cool this hour of the night, rushing up your legs. You feel strange. You feel powerful. You want to laugh in his face. You want to tell him you're not for sale. But before you can, he gets up and leaves.

Whatever. The manager comes back and sits down next to you without saying a word.

—These pills are really fucking me up.

Say it as if this will explain everything: why you are here, waiting for your Quaalude to kick in at a freezing, nearly empty bar with slides of naked children for sale projected above your head, talking to a man who is leaving it all tomorrow to become a monk.

I am in a taxi going to the airport. I could go back to Thong's and eat dinner, but the prospect of being in the same house as that creepy maid is a little too real for me right now, plus it's too early to go to Patpong, so I take a cab to the airport, which at night is about a forty-minute ride from the city, and hang around watching music videos in the lounge and study the flights that are returning or leaving for Burma, for Dhaka, for Hong Kong, for Swatow, for Chiang Mai, wondering whether I should just get on one and call it quits and cut my losses, but I don't. What I do is go to the bathroom and lock the stall door and finish up another half gram of something that feels far too speedy to be called coke and burns my nose. Then I turn around at exactly midnight and get a cab to Patpong. The driver floors it as soon as we leave the curb, and soon we're flying down the expressway. His hands leave the wheel when we pass Wat Laksi and his head inclines slightly, momentarily, and then he's back in control of his little Peugeot hurtling through space. I pull out a cigarette and offer him one, which he takes, and then he looks at me through the rearview mirror and asks me if it's my first time in Thailand.

—You idiot. *Khrap kheu khon Thai.*

His eyes turn up to the rearview mirror.

—*You don't look it.*

I light my cigarette and don't offer him the lighter.

He tucks the cigarette behind his ear and studies the traffic moving at a frightening clip around us.

—You have a friend in Thailand?

—Brother, I have a fucking family in Thailand.

He's quiet for a few miles. Smiling throughout.

—Do you like girls?

Second drag of cigarette. Look at him closely before exhaling. He's not bad-looking. Early twenties. Nice haircut. He asks again.

—Do you like boys?

—I like you.

He smiles and looks at me again in the mirror. Differently this time.

We leave the hotel together at around 3 A.M., and my driver friend leaves me at the corner of Silom and Surawong. Two drag queens are sitting on the bench outside of Robinson's when I walk past. One has on a purple turban that looks like it's made of some really uncomfortable synthetic material. The other one is wearing heavy blue eye shadow which doesn't do much for her. Purple Turban has a cigarette in her mouth, barely, and a book of matches resting in her hand. Blue Eye Shadow is frantically trying to pry the matches from her fingers so she can light Purple Turban's cigarette.

—Uh-uh. No. Uh-uh. Now you in my personal space.

Purple Turban says it without moving a muscle. If there is a nation outside of this city I have forgotten it. If there is a single field of rice that exists outside of this district of three parallel private streets I can now call mine, it was a lie told to sell a package tour. These three streets differentiated in name only by digits. Patpong Neung. Patpong Song. Patpong Sarm. But every red-light district is a story of digits.

1946: A Teochew businessman, Udom Patpong, buys this parcel of land for 59,000 baht. His son, returning from the University of Minnesota, develops the land for foreign business offices. 1956: The first massage parlor opens to service Japanese businessmen. 1969: R&R. 1965: Thanom Kittikachorn and Praphas Charasthien military putsch. 1972: Napalm. 1972: Semen. 1972: Cash. 1975: The liberation of Saigon. 1976: Tourism.

A middle-aged man, his pink skin peeling off inside a white button-down shirt, strides purposefully through the nighttime chaos of Silom. He is carrying a gym bag, the sides emblazoned with the logo for the U.S. Military Academy. I can't say what this man is doing here: businessman, tourist, torturer, Mr. America, or Miss Military Adviser. Whatever. It's not like he doesn't somehow fit in, but his sense of purpose this evening is somewhat elusive. Even to him. I can see it on his face. Those furrows of confusion.

A motorcycle lurches onto the sidewalk, frustrated by the deadened flow of traffic on Silom. The driver cuts close behind Mr. America. He turns around, his gym bag flying.

—Drive on the fucking street!

He yells in a trademark Minnesota curl. Passersby turn their heads. Pretend they don't hear him. The cyclist smiles. It is a thin, vaguely embarrassed smile.

—Drive on the fucking street!

The man punches the driver for emphasis. The driver nearly falls off his bike but manages to catch himself in time to see Miss Military Adviser strut off. The driver revs his engine, speeds up a few meters until he is at Mr. America's heels. Mr. America turns, his fists clenched.

—Drive on the fucking street!

As if by repeating the exact same five words, he can reorder the universe.

A mild rage, unreasonable and futile, tickles my throat. I scan the throng of pedestrians choking Silom for sympathy, but no one else seems to have noticed this confrontation. Even the motorcyclist has disappeared. Fury melts into a low-grade sorrow. I'm overcome with something. Some need. Maybe it's the need to feel pity for Miss Military Adviser. Or the need to fuck him senseless. In this city, every potential for war becomes a potential for a caress. In this city that desires nothing more than the movement it has lost, our bodies intersect and embrace at every corner. Yet for Mr. America, these encounters can only be obstacles. Space is not something to be shared or transformed through presence, but a place to own. For Mr. America, every movement forward is a step into a land empty of people. Vacant, wasted, and unused. Ripe for development. A step across a city that was never planned for life.

America passes me on his way down Silom. I make it a point to match his stare, peer into his eyes, and catch a piece of something unpleasant and familiar. I watch him turn into Soi 2, his body once again lumbering down the alley with the arrogance of a murderer. His body. The prospect of order and civilization. My body. The obstacle to its linear progression. But these two bodies are merely intimate explanations of each other. History is as trapped in both our bodies as our bodies are trapped in history. What happens to that legacy when the body breaks? What happens to the part of us that cannot concede that anything is impossible? That part will go on to master the universe. Burn whole libraries of truth to write history. Anything but accept impotence, mortality, and limitation.

I watch Miss Military Adviser loiter in front of a cabaret doorway. *Very sexy show,* the barker promises him. *No cover charge.* His steps mimic a journey of historic purpose. The search for the fountain of youth. The tonic to arrest the course of flesh. Flesh too transient to fix a price. Flesh that falls like space from the borders of the grid that attempts to define it. Flesh with no worth beyond life. Life in the pitch of cinemas, bathhouses, public toilets, park bushes, underneath banyan trees. When that life recedes it reveals bones that are as white and colorless as ghosts. Angels with skin that cuts like razors. As white and colorless as the monster inside me.

Late one afternoon in 1824, as the Scottish trader Robert Hunter was returning to his house on the west bank of the Chao Phraya, he was struck by an extraordinary sight before him in the water. It was a creature that appeared to have two heads, four arms, and four legs, all of which were moving in perfect harmony. As Hunter watched, the object climbed into a nearby boat, and to his amazement he realized that he had been looking at two small boys who were joined together at the waist. Chang and Eng, as the boys were named, were then thirteen years old, the sons of a Nyonya mother and a Teochew father, and they were bought by Hunter, who shipped them off to America to work the sideshows of P. T. Barnum's circus. The twins wound up becoming naturalized American citizens, changed their name to Bunker, married plantation belles, and lived in the American South during antebellum slavery. One of their children even fought on the side of the Confederacy. One ever feels their twoness. Like twin circuits in a machine. In the mess but not of it. Implicit and resistant. Acquired and interred in a story we never wrote. The narrative of humanity. The narrative of civilization. The narrative of air-conditioning in the tropics. The narrative of heaven, from which the dark-skinned children of paradise fell. The most banal and unattainable paradise. A shopping mall where only the commodity has rights. To embrace all the flavor the World Bank is offering this season it is necessary to reduce space to place and time to minutes. To devour the twin fruits of original sin. To believe that progress moves like a dumb tourist in a straight line of alabaster conquest.

—Nurse! Nurse!

I call Muk over to the counter of the Milk Bar. Slip her two wrinkled 500-baht notes. She salutes me, eyes lowered, and raises a silver tray to the counter. On it there is my change and a pink packet, bundled with a finger of Scotch tape. I pick up the cash first, fold it in my wallet, take a single-edged razor from behind my Visa card, and slice open the packet. Concentrate on chopping its contents up into a fine crystal talc. I don't bother going into the tiny, barely functioning bathroom in the back. I don't even offer a deferential bump to any of the highborn patrons I barely know sitting around me, as they have done too many nights before this. Too noble to even register their disdain, they merely turn their eyes, avert their conversations. I take a plastic straw from a jar on the bar. Without looking, Muk takes it from my hands and snips off the end with a scissor. She hands it back to me, not even bothering to look at me as I inhale line after line into this odorless funnel. When did our kisses betray our true lust? When did they become a means of consumption?

Open the mouth. The nose. The vein. Devour through every pore.

—*Did you hear what happened to Boi?*

— . . .

—*He went home with some guy he met at Harry's last night. Said he was a doctor. Boi thought he had scored big. They went to some hotel. The next thing he knows, he wakes up in some hotel bathtub, packed in ice, with one kidney gone.*

—. . .

—*The doctor left a phone next to the tub with a note.*

—. . .

—*He's in the hospital now.*

From the window of the bar I watch the go-go dancer who grabbed my crotch yesterday morning walk out into the middle of Silom, her eyes so blank and glossy cars could drive through them. But instead they screech and swerve to miss her. A driver in a short-sleeve powder-blue shirt yells out the window. Asks her if she values her life.

—Where do good go-go dancers go when they die?

Muk barely looks up. Stirs her drink with her fingers. The first go-go dancer was introduced here in 1969 by a U.S. Air Force mechanic. Little Brown Fucking Machine. A body that is really the sum of its organic functions. Consume. Assimilate. Incubate. Excrete. A scientific system of potential services. Bite. Suck. Devour. Shit. All obscuring the body's real emptiness.

From here it is only a nighttime away to the place where my father passed away. Tonight his collapsing body covers the sky, shuddering each breath. I sit at a table outside the Milk Bar and order a pitcher of margaritas. I need to impair my judgment. Which exotic disease of the tropics claimed my child-beating father? Malaria? Dengue? Yellow fever? Cholera? All the inoculations were in order. Cirrhosis of the liver, more likely. Alcoholism. Overwork, fear, inferiority complexes, addiction, trepidation, servility, despair, abasement. Broken shadows, hair overgrown and trembling in the cup of his nostrils. Quiet hysteria growing in the flickering glow of his cramped apartment in Honolulu. Surrounded by all the television sets and useless technology he had acquired over his broken life. Brown stains. Ashen legs. Smell of sweat, emptied vodka, and yeast lingering idle inside his body for fifty-three years, three months, and eighteen days. I can taste the night-blooming jasmine from the forest outside. The perfume of turmoil. *Help me*. Toothless gums, barely pink. *Help me*. Itchiness. *I want to*— He doesn't finish the sentence. I help him to the toilet. There is no need. There is only the odor of abjection and not the act itself. I help him back to his cot. My hand is wild and warm in his. *My child*. The only time he ever called me that. The night he died I fell asleep without crying. I dreamed I woke up the next morning, and the whole city was burned to the ground.

I leave the bar, walk down the alley to the curb of Silom. There is a taxi driver leaning against his car with an unlit cigarette in his hand.

—My father was a good man.

Without missing a beat he asks me what that means, *good*. I shrug, walk through rows of idle traffic. Unseasonable winds caress my face. Waxy smell of death sweet underneath my fingernails.

Muk tells me there was never any sound more satisfying to hear than the crunch of a drunken GI's head breaking on the streets of Pattaya. This was back in the sixties. She had been walking back to her hotel when she heard a loud groan and thud. When she turned she saw a six-foot-six U.S. marine in shorts and one of those *I may not go down in history but I will go down on your sister* T-shirts crumple to the street. Within seconds he was surrounded by several bouncers from nearby bars, who poked him to see if he was still alive and, when they found he was, started kicking his head in. You could hear the wet crunch of their boots down the street. One of them picked his head up and started smacking it down on to the asphalt. Even from where Muk was standing she could see blood and snot flying off the street. She had never heard anything so affirming as the delighted cries of the bar girls watching all this from the sidewalks of their go-go clubs, screaming for vengeance. But before they could finish the job, a stream of soldiers came running out of one of the bars to rescue their fallen comrade. There was a lively pitched battle between these tall overdeveloped GIs and the wiry bar bouncers that lasted until the police van pulled up to arrest people. But, like I said, this was back in the sixties. Before we had a Tourism Authority. When our roles in the game were much more clear. When you knew who your friends were.

You stay out until after sunup, have a bowl of *sen yai* at a noodle stand, as administrative assistants and bankers spring by on their way to work. An old woman in a head wrap and sarong hobbles up to you silently and sticks out her hand without saying a word. You put a few coins in it, thinking how fucking predictable this is getting.

—Why don't you do something to surprise me.

You say it probably a little too bitterly. But mother has that seen-it-all-before look that glues her features into an immobile, inexpressive mask.

—*Shut up, you poor excuse for a white woman.*

She hisses it in what should be your dialect, then closes her fist around those heavy coins and walks off, completely unimpressed. You waste some time in a bookstore on Silom before you finally grab a taxi home, sucking back your snot trying to taste the night before, your teeth grinding in long concentric circles. His sister says Thong's got a guest. She makes a face. Dirty.

It's dark downstairs. Your bare feet land on something hard and powerful. It's the gold ring you bought Thong. Still radiant, it glows enough to illuminate two forms crumpled in bed. One is a woman. You want to wake her up. You want to see your replacement. You want to turn and run in terror. Instead, you put the ring on the table by the bed and content yourself with her high, whistling snore.

You need someone to talk to, even though you know everybody is sick of hearing about Thong. Sick of hearing you whine. You call Luk's apartment. He's checked out suddenly. Left no address. The woman at the other end sounds confused. Thinks he left the country. You call Luk's office. No answer.

Luk's northern hotel collapsed. Just like that. There one minute. And the next: just a cloud of dust. The newscaster's face is dark, matte, handsome. His jaundiced neck wrapped in a white collar and tie. You watch transfixed from the couch. The sounds emerging. You watch the words form in his mouth. Travel across space and time before they reach you. You turn them over like toys. Each one. Sorting them. The tones. High. Middle. Falling. Rising. Low. You absentmindedly crack open a rambutan from a plastic bag of them on the floor. You are not surprised to find it has gone bad. A movement of tactile assaults: sour, stinking, fuchsia, and hairy. You hold the elements wet and putrid on your fingertips, watching the bodies pulled from the rubble. One in particular catches your eye. A mutilated body. Particularly mutilated. The skin falling off the cheeks in sheaves.

His name is Wongchai Puanmuanpak. His nickname is a splinter of concrete at the bottom of the collapsed hotel. His testimony is a collage of fragmented sentences delivered on national television.

—*I used the blood from my head as ink to write a message to my beloved. Trapped in a small corner I was forced to sit. One man was hit by a slab of concrete and lay writhing in my lap. He died in a few minutes.*

Later. After the search teams have given up and forgotten the names of the missing. After the grounds have been sprinkled with jasmine perfume and blessed by brahmins. After the ministries in question have been pardoned. After the families of the dead and injured have each been given 2500 baht to shut up. Long after you have forgotten the name of the northern hotel and the sight of the corpses on the news you will remember the number of bodies pulled from the debris: 147. You will remember even after you have forgotten what 147 means. You will buy lottery tickets with it. You will lay bets on it.

★ ★ ★

His stepmother goes down the steps to the basement. From the living room you can hear shouting above the television. Secretly you are pleased and hope it doesn't show on your face. You hear footsteps. More shouting. A woman's voice. Inflamed. Obstreperous.

A door slamming. You look out the window and see the back of a woman stepping quickly out the front gate. When she looks around the street you can see that she is, honestly, very beautiful.

A few minutes later you hear a man's voice. His father. His tone makes the skin across your back shuffle and flush. You have heard this sound before. Lazy. Good-for-nothing. Waste. Trash. Say the word *father*. Now say the word *son*. Universal intonation. You say the first with a clenched jaw. The second in tears. You hear Thong crying now. It is the second time you have heard him cry. More voices now. His stepmother's voice. Try the word *mother*. Sapphire martini in a chilled glass. You will pretend not to understand the language you hear rumbling from the other room, even though it tastes as old and familiar as the words tripping off your tongue. *Ba. Ma.* Mommy. Daddy. You exist only to ruin them.

They have left you alone with Thong. Gone shopping. Left you both alone in this big house at the edge of the *muban*. Nothing but the locusts and waving weeds this Sunday afternoon. You console him best you know how. Pitifully. Give him a glass of water. You would give him some coke if you had any left. Tell him to calm down. Tell him about your own father.

—And look at me now.

He laughs. Viciously. There is a long quiet. Then finally he says it.

—This is just a vacation for you, isn't it?

You don't answer. In the end, you are just an American darker than the rest, doing things in Thailand you can never do at home. This makes you invincible. So invincible that you think he can hurt you as much as he wants, you just don't want him to leave.

But later, fortified with the night, you regain what you mistake as your dignity. You find the ring you gave him where you left it, on the bedside table, and slip it into your pocket. *Fuck you,* you tell him. You've got your own life. You don't need him.

—Fuck you.
—*You got to have a dick to do that, baby.*

—Don't even smile at me, bitch. I'll cut it off your face.
—I'm leaving.

—Aren't you going to stop me?

You know the shape of his body in the dark. Your fingers tumble over his skin, desperate to find a flaw, any flaw that will betray his humanity. Instead, there is his face that inspires a thousand plane tickets, a million visa bribes. The more you know him the uglier you become. His arms ascend poverty. You will build your love on a lie. A lie so beautiful even you will forget it's pure fiction. Once upon a time, he whispered how much he loved you so often that it started to sound as natural as wind.

You call the airline. There are still seats on the plane back to New York the next day. Flights to Hong Kong every few hours. Tokyo. Taipei. Dubai. Beirut. Berlin. Los Angeles. Flights to anywhere. The world is yours.

Interior. Evening. Your room in Pratunam. You're alone again. Tomorrow morning, before the city rises en masse and suffocates the ruined streets, you'll hail a taxi on Thanon Ratchaparop and head to the airport. You will ask the driver how much the fare is, and no matter what he says you'll pay it. The airport. That's the only destination you have in mind right now. After that is just a premonition. But you're ready to go. Anywhere. You've finished packing. Underwear. Some shirts. Jeans. You are not surprised that the contents of your life fit in one carry-on bag. You are not surprised at much these days.

You go to the pharmacy and ask for something to get you through the night. Something different, you say. He shows you a thin wafer the color of milk. *Rohypnol*. He draws out each syllable to make sure you understand. *A memory killer*. He smiles. The will to endless circulation. No prescription necessary. He happily counts out six of them with a short metal scepter. You will remember nothing. His promise slaps your back on the way out. At the *satay* stand down the street, you pick up a bottle of Maekhong. Inside your room, you fix yourself a little cocktail to wash down the Rohypnol. The solution eases into your tangled body, a lovely whisper to put you out.

Some things you notice in the dun moments before closing
your eyes:

The view from the tiny porch: The buses idling in early
evening traffic on the superhighway. There are boys dancing inside the buses. You can hear the song from across the muddy yard.
It's on the radio all the time. Everyone knows it that season.

The shower, with shattered glass on the tiles from the bottle
of whiskey you dropped.

The lazy air conditioner.

The Panasonic color television, playing *A Touch of Evil*. Janet
Leigh is still struggling against the inevitable.

The cheap bed. The one with the pastel-colored frame that
looks like it's made of plastic.

The mirror with the cruel overhead fluorescent light,
humming.

Okay, Miss Citizen of the World. Since you're so good at
history, do you remember what city it was that I last shared my
body with you? Where was it? Come on, you know where it
was. Some ugly city with great promise. New York, probably.
Maybe Paris. No. No. It's here. The City of Angels. You're sitting here with me now, baby. Just the two of us. You look
familiar. Like someone who has been with me all along. Someone who has survived the trip intact. You've made it. Let's cele-
brate. I lie back naked on the bed and you carefully empty a
gram of pure heaven onto my body. You take care to shape the
powder into long white ski trails along the slopes of my arms.
Chest. Legs. A skinny collection of sharp turns that flattens into
a mirror of itself. You and I.

Go ahead. You first. I don't need much to get off. To lose myself. To just hand my body over. Freeing me to float away. Your face travels the cold expanse of my body. Inhaling. Devouring. Bringing the surface inside. Becoming your need. Your hand smooths the flesh out underneath.

Look intently at the roads crossing underneath my skin, a fantasy of order snaking out from my heart. You thought this was something in which you wouldn't have to participate. Thought this was a story you could just watch unravel. A consuming stain that stops short of where you're standing.

No.

Something else is happening as you stretch around me. Hold me. Tight. You are looking me over. Searching me for some kind of closure. The end of a journey. I'm sorry I can't oblige. My extended arms will always form the perimeter of an open sore. Even as you bring the wound to your thin, even mouth. Kiss it.

—I love you.

I can barely hear your nasal voice.

—I love you because your body is expensive.

I feel many things as you spread over me. Into me. Geese flying in a V-formation across the night sky. The sound the moon makes completing its arc. Your blood sneaking back into the chamber of your heart. The open door of every consciousness. A plane streaks toward a place I've only heard of before. Somewhere. A city where a familiar language crackles on the pavement. I've heard its songs. Their meanings beat against a fading alarm. Five A.M. It's almost time to go. My eyes brace against a white dawn. Fireflies light the way home.

Hutang emas dapat dibayar
Hutang budi dibawa mati.
A debt of gold can be repaid
A favor is cherished forever.

Ira Silverberg, Harold Schmidt, Elizabeth Schambelan, Charles Woods, Toby Chuah, Andrew Chuah Ah Bah, Jacob Chuah and family, Shu Lea Cheang, John Letourneau, Paul Pfeiffer, Christian Haye, bell hooks, Jessica Hagedorn, Brigitte Landou, Michael Hornburg, Ooi Kok Hong, Kim Soo Kyung, and Virapong Kongpradith: Thank you.

Grateful acknowledgment is also made to the New York Foundation for the Arts, the Banff Centre for the Arts, and Villa Montalvo for their generous support during the writing of this book.